'Lucy Ellmann's delightfully dotty novel is a fantastical flight across life, death and the universe ... Ellmann's style is irreverently batty, charged with such infectious, frequently angry energy that it is no wonder she often feels the need to SHOUT' *Daily Telegraph*

'One of the funniest, most mordant and perfectly formed books I've read' Ali Smith, author of *Hotel World*

'Ellmann writes with the knowingness and authority of someone who has plumbed the depths of despair and come up laughing – hysterically' *The Times*

'A bizarre and blackly entertaining universe ... Ellmann's satiric intent is honed and deadly' *Image*

'Lucy Ellmann should by rights become a household name ... a strange, profound, bittersweet comedy ... Funny and provocative, this is one of the most unusual books you're likely to read all year' *Sainsbury's Magazine*

'Ellmann's solution to Dot's terrible knowledge makes this a raging, funny book' *Marie Claire*

'It's the kind of novel you don't want to read alone, in silence, which is infuriating for any poor soul who wanders into the room only to be grabbed and read the good bits' *Guardian*

D0995334

DOT IN THE UNIVERSE

LUCY ELLMANN

BLOOMSBURY

Technical information was gathered from several sources,
including Sebastian Junger's *The Perfect Storm*.

First published 2003
This paperback edition published in 2004

Copyright © 2003 by Lucy Ellmann

The moral right of the author
has been asserted

Bloomsbury Publishing Plc, 38 Soho Square,
London WID 3HB

A CIP catalogue record for this book
is available from the British Library

ISBN 0 7475 6803 0

10 9 8 7 6 5 4 3 2 1

All paper used by Bloomsbury Publishing, including that in this
book is a natural, recyclable product made from wood grown in
sustainable, well-managed forests. The manufacturing processes
conform to the environmental regulations of the country of origin.

Typeset by Palimpsest Book Production Limited,
Polmont, Stirlingshire

Printed in Great Britain by Clays Ltd, St Ives plc

www.bloomsbury.com/lucyellmann

For Todd McEwen

PART ONE

There is a pleasure in the pathless woods,
There is a rapture on the lonely shore.

Byron

DOT ON THE HORIZON

When surveying a landscape you imagine yourself GOD. You long to pat the clumpy tops of trees, turn rivers with a muddy palm, cup hills and, stretching out, caress an entire abdomenlike valley. Tiny despots in a universe too BIG for us, we tower over things, but other things tower over US. I've always wanted to be able to fly, about twenty feet up. I'd just like to get a good LOOK at things. We're held so tightly to the earth.

Dot Butser was flying, but not happily. She was crawling up the aisle of a plane that had hit a spell of 'turbulence'. Dot was returning to her hubby who had earlier fainted, apparently DIED, after eating too many jalapeño peppers at the airport. Not long after the plane took off, he'd CONKED OUT. Dot had screamed for assistance, which resulted in four stewardesses administering oxygen to John and a Kleenex and a glass of water to Dot, who was crying. It was this water that Dot was PEEING OUT when 'turbulence' struck. She emerged from the loo to find everyone else safely strapped in, except one other woman who was also crawling along the floor. But SHE soon got to her seat; Dot had a lot further to go.

This is HELL, thought Dot. I will be forced to exchange FAREWELL GLANCES with STRANGERS, I am going to die clinging to this musty little avenue of carpet instead of my lovely HUBBY, whose cheeks so please me, whose cock is so thick, I crawl to him!

When she finally reached him, John was READING. The plane's shifts from air pocket to pressure front, swaying like a CAMEL not a plane, merely made him CROSS. Dot clambered over him, satisfied that at least now they would die together, yelling endearments and shitting themselves in adjacent seats.

A MIRACLE, is it not, that two people, unrelated, can meet and mean so much to each other? Yet coupledom is taken for granted. The whole world organises itself around the fact that people manage to get their awkward bodies in position to FUCK, an achievement honoured by toasters, tandems and tax cuts. How nice, how CONVE-NIENT heterosexuality is. You may not even have met the guy yet but already useful items are being made for you: a two-door sedan or an electric underblanket with two sets of controls. Complete STRANGERS know that you'll want to share meals, beds, homes, even a burial plot, that you will long for each other's touch and seek to exclude others. The intimacy and anarchy of it all!

'This is the worst flight I've ever been on,' Dot informed John. He nodded. They both stared at the screens in front of them. Each seat had its own individual TV screen stuck on the back of the seat in front, so that everyone could watch their own individual choice of CRAP as they flew to their DOOM. Dot couldn't even find anything to watch. She stared out of the window.

The sun rose suddenly, much too FAST, missing out on the best bit, when time creaks on its hinges: twilight. It is such BULLSHIT that you can see nice sunsets from planes, the aurora borealis, UFOs, whatever. Nothing you see from a plane MATTERS. I once saw the entire ARCTIC CIRCLE from a plane, for HOURS, hundreds and hundreds of miles of cracked ice gradually turning blue as the sun went down. I searched it for Inuit. But none of this COUNTS. To really feel you've been to the North Pole you've got to TRUDGE, with sleighs and huskies, troublesome companions and weird food-stuffs. You've got to get frostbite. In fact you've got to be an IDIOT. There's a REASON why such places are uninhabited:

How did we all get so AMBULANT anyway? (In our flight socks!) Everybody's two-week holiday is now spent being shot through the air to some sunny spot, the more distant the more impressed your pals will be. You don't have time to learn the LANGUAGE or really get to KNOW anybody or even digest your FOOD before you're back at your desk with your festering insect bites, the office sandwich and intrigues, abundant tea with milk, reliable loos and a GP who has your records (if he could only FIND them). Your cat, all unknowing about Lanzarote or the Seychelles, still needs feeding at 7:00 on the dot. How is any of this more meaningful than the life of a BUG? They too get around.

5

Dot and John were herded like SHEEP off the plane, but regained some individuality when they located John's car and set off for Jaywick. Jaywick in January. A deserted holiday camp echoing with furious family fun (long past) is all that separates Jaywick Sands from Clacton-on-Sea which is not far from Colchester where you used to get OYSTERS and Queen Boadicea but NOT ANY MORE. Originally conceived as a low-cost summer retreat for car-factory workers, Jaywick was subsequently taken over by ill-judging old folk like John's grandmother (who'd left her house to him).

You'd THINK a house with a sea view must be redeemable but you'd be wrong: there was something terrible about that big grey sea whenever you got a glimpse of it. Nobody in Jaywick wanted anything to DO with the sea! They huddled behind their mile of concrete sea wall righting garden gnomes, mending miniature picket fences and replacing the quotation marks on their house plaques ("Casa Blanca", "Starfish Vista", "Hydra Hideaway"), their damp stucco and buggered begonias no match for the salt spray off the North Sea.

John tootled happily up Broadway with its boarded-up bucket 'n' spade shops and defunct hair salon, then on to Sea Cornflower Way, turning left on Sea Rosemary Way, right on Sea Lavender Way, right again on Sea Thistle Way, then zoomed down Morris Minor Avenue. Dot was getting quite a tour of her new neighbourhood! After Ford Motorola Boulevard they headed east and finally reached Abalone Avenue where John's house stood: "Oceania".

John picked Dot up and carried her to the front door, giving her a quick glimpse of the garden. On some propitious day of bachelorhood John had planted two little birch trees which had so far survived their tussles with the wind, perhaps because they were still so small. The rest consisted of shells, dead crabs, ice-lolly wrappers, a prostrate dustbin and a slice of red lace clinging to a shrub.

After letting Dot into the house, John raced off to the chip shop (one of the few businesses willing to brave the Jaywick winter). Dot surveyed her humble home. There were no obvious comforts, apart from a tall pile of *Scientific Americans* stacked against a wall. A layer of sand on everything seemed to speak of a secret happier life the house led when unoccupied, as if it had never reconciled itself to human habitation. EVERYTHING in Jaywick is hostile to human habitation. Jaywick just wants to be mere and grey again. It doesn't know what people are DOING there, with their sea-thistle ways and their salt-and-vinegar chips, their cars nosing through storms and their deep stupid fear of the sea. Jaywick doesn't see the point.

Dot stood in the middle of this unwelcoming scene and thought, I want to DRINK him, SWIM in him. He could KILL me and I'd like it. I would let him shit in my hand! How I need just to be near him.

She loved to watch him talk: she loved the light in his eyes. Maybe everyone has a light in their eyes when they talk, but these were JOHN's eyes, John's mouth. She loved to TOUCH him, meet his hips with hers, roll her fingers in the groove of his spine. She loved his hands, his chin, his chest, his LOWER LIP.

7

She loved his manliness, and he her womanliness: they fitted together according to the usual fashion. It's not our FAULT we got the idea we could UNITE, that we might not be forever all alone in the world – fucking is very suggestive of merging.

John returned with two fish suppers but they didn't eat them. Some fish DIED for them, got FRIED for them, but they didn't care. They were too busy KISSING. Dot knelt before John and put his hard cock into her warm red mouth. He turned her. John loved Dot's ASS, liked to see her bending over, liked to clutch her ass and spank it and fuck her from behind. This now left Dot staring at a dull corner of the unfamiliar living room, but she concentrated on the animal nature of the act and her own feral position in it and was content. She trembled as he opened her legs. She gripped the mantelpiece but kept sinking with pleasure to the floor. John pulled her back up and fucked her some more.

A young couple with no real impediments to happiness, basking in calm seas without worry or care! But who can contain and order the rampages of the human heart, its desires and despair? Love, like defecation, is never a settled matter. It forms and re-forms itself, makes itself felt, makes itself a NUISANCE. Merely a vehicle for physical exchange with another – illogical to place so much importance on it.

Such a hideous species after all, so unprepossessingly UPRIGHT, gangly, and so BARE (fur or feathers would have helped, or a pronounced canine SNOUT), the only thing distinguishing one from another: gestures, habits, hairlines, like OLD SHOES moulded to your particular shape – take 'em all down to the charity shop!

What does it matter what we DO or what becomes of us, flesh and bone that moves and thinks for a while and then cuts out? What does it matter what we THOUGHT? Does it even matter if you DIE? A few people will notice and then they'll die too! Life continues around the deathbed itself – people must EAT. Nothing is left of you but a sour voice in your daughter's head every time she loses her keys, or an empty seat on the bus – and there are MORE BRIOCHES for everybody!

Hungry in the middle of the night, hopeless too, alone or not, always alone really, Dot gets up. John's back against hers in the bed is not enough. She is full of FEAR, a conduit for emotions that come with their own INTEN-SITY, their own intent. Raw, violent life-or-death stuff! She doesn't RECOGNISE herself. She wants to DIE or KILL, for fear of how much she cares about him. And why not? In a world so full of death, the law against murder seems an arbitrary whim.

Eating a stale cracker, Dot returns to her lover's arms beneath the eiderdown. Outside, the two birch trees stand rigid in the wind. Muscular and gleaming like dancers' legs, they barely connect with the ground. The DRAMA of it all! The passing cars don't know what's going on in these trees.

DOT ON THE CARPET

John liked Dot in a tight corset with her breasts and ass bulging out above and below. He liked tying her with silken cords while murmuring in her ear – tying, teasing and taking her. Dot was never happier than when helpless, bound by her wrists and ankles to the bed! With corsets, kimonos, stockings, suspender belts, camisoles, wigs, tassels, vagina balls, high heels, blindfolds, handcuffs, and an all-rubber French Maid outfit, Dot and John attempted to contain and order the rampages of the human heart.

John was pleased with his pretty wifey. She reminded him of his MOTHER, whom he hadn't seen for many years. John's mother lived in Switzerland. Her influence on John was minimal – she might as well have been on the MOON (in fact he only thought of her about twelve times a year). He was amazed to have found Dot and her sudden abundant LOVE, a woman willing to be with him anywhere, any time.

Dot had the perfect face for her era: tight-lipped, pointy-nosed, pink-skinned, blonde-haired. MOST

WOMEN IN ENGLAND CURRENTLY LOOK LIKE THIS. It is the face that has WON THE DAY. Jill Dando, Mariella Frostrup, Zoë Ball, Anthea Turner, Julia Somerville, Ffion, Sophie, and that rugby player's ex-wife* (his next one looked just the SAME). All would-be DIANAS, the dumb blank eyes perfectly offset by the sharp nose-and-chin combo, fake innocence seamlessly shading into utter indifference. It's the look of all TV presenters and PR people, and no doubt the look they advise in OTHERS: it's photogenic and low-maintenance, the short hair undisturbed by a swimming, skiing, airport press conference, neck massage, blow-job lifestyle – and it goes so well with a dark-haired boyfriend!

But Dot had something that set her apart from all the other Dots and Ffions, a Fatal Flaw (everyone should have one). She hid it rather well but it was a great SHAME, an UGLINESS, which put a damper on things and filled her, when she let it, with despair. (AND IT WOULD DO THE SAME TO YOU IF YOU HAD IT.)

Dot modelled her life on American SCHLOCK, those TV movies about women who suffer and solve things. Men play only rapists, ineffectual bosses and exasperated husbands in these dramas. It is always the WOMAN, stubborn, maligned and well toned, who wrestles the judicial system to the ground or SAVES LIVES or in some other way TRIUMPHS OVER ALL. There is comfort in the myth of the Lone Woman. You think YOU'VE got problems until you spend three hours watching a TV movie

* Julia Carling.

11

about a nice scientist lady who never hurt a fly (except in the vivisection lab) but finds out one day that her dead son has been cloned EIGHT TIMES without her knowledge or consent. Now that's TROUBLE. She has to drive through many leafy suburbs and approach petty officialdom with WILD BESEECHING EYES before she can correct this moral outrage and reinstate perfection throughout America.

But it wasn't the plots that obsessed Dot. It was the spick-and-span KITCHEN COUNTERS, the self-sufficient GOLDFISH, the SPAGHETTI that hadn't moved from its JAR for years. Not a pubic hair out of place, all bodily functions approved by the sponsors and the decor plagiarised from hotel chains. You need very little in a place like that, having done away with desire, dread and disappointment. No pain, no paperwork, only yourself to worry about and YOU'RE a well-groomed DOT IN THE UNIVERSE.

Dots abound in the universe. Sheep shit nice little black dots, ladybugs shit the tiniest. Dot's OWN shit sometimes came out in dots. Drips are really dots, as are tears and raindrops, atoms and molecules, cells, nuclei, dust particles. The sun and stars and, intermittently, the moon. Roses on watering cans. Gum on the pavement, and those little metal discs nobody knows the meaning of. Sparkles from sparklers, sprinkles from sprinklers, and vice versa. The Japanese flag. Spots on birds, frogs, dogs, butterflies and leopards. Speckles on eggs and feathers and fruit and flowers, and the little white dots on the rumps of fawns. Buds, buttons, berries, beetles, barley, balls, beads, beans, burrs, berets, buckshot, BRAILLE. Poppy seeds, cherry tomatoes, chocolate chips, currants, raisins, zeros, umlauts, periods, decimal points, coins, egg yolks, musical notation, Seurat, radar, the dots on dominoes or dice, hail, snow-flakes, hubcaps, headlights, tumbleweed, lighthouse beacons, portholes, buoys, limpets, pearls and other jewels. Pupils, irises, painted toe-nails, ear-rings, nose-rings and tongue studs, pimples, dimples, nipples and nostrils, pores, pox, the mouths of surprised or singing people, vaginas, assholes and the upholstery work of stomach and rib-cage held together by the button we ALL have. The EARTH is a dot from far enough away.

Dot in the universe. Dot was insignificant, but who isn't? So much EFFORT we put into life, all the feeding, clothing, educating, medicating, fornicating, masturbating, cleansing and conversing. All the ANXIETY. When it really doesn't matter if a single person gets happy. The universe DOESN'T GIVE A DAMN.

THE RATTY TEA COSIES
OF JAYWICK SANDS

Dot lived for John, and John for Dot. He was the man for her, and she the woman for him (it's important to get these things the right way round). He was so NICELY MADE (as was she). But they were conducting their idyll in JAYWICK SANDS, the arsehole of the universe! Though Jaywick opens and shuts itself annually, it farts away its future without regard. So it came to pass that the outside world INTRUDED on Dot and John, and the inner world was allowed to sort of POP OUT: a hernia of cosmic proportions ensued.

For one thing, there were a hell of a lot of old ladies milling about out there. John had only just rid "Oceania" of old-lady clutter when Dot arrived. He had shorn it, driven it back down to the bare boards and sand it was meant to be, tamed the jungle of old-lady equipment and paraphernalia with his scythe (and plenty of rubbish bags). Out with the comfy crap of his grandma's arthritic end. In its place, the clear straight lines of wood and metal that gathered the dust of MANHOOD that mollified John.

Outside, the two birch trees he'd planted: sturdy straight lines, like John himself.

But John had an address book full of old ladies' names (friends of his grandma) and Dot ended up having tea with them all when John was out on the boat. Dot would clip their toe-nails and listen to their bubbling memories of husbands (long-gone) and children (ungrateful) and THINGS, icky glass paperweights, china balls of flowers, crocheted head-rests, eyesores from Mysore.

As a result, Dot developed her own taste for junk and started foraging in the junk shops of Essex. She would descend on the shop, quickly evaluate stuff in her own way, assigning meaning indiscriminately, until she found something, ANYTHING, to buy. She feared the junk-shop owners, sitting like GODS amongst their junk: they alone knew what it was and where it all came from.

Without even asking him, Dot had assumed John wanted their windswept bungalow to have an ENGLISH COTTAGE FEEL, and set about creating this with porcelain, pewter and chintz (it would have been simpler to buy mismatched furniture and just let the damp set in). She learnt how to incorporate her junk-shop finds into "Oceania" by reading the style section in the back pages of Sunday newspapers, and became ADDICTED to the advice of Belinda Lurcher who had her own TV SHOW. Belinda Lurcher's ideas, often involving bun moss balls, were never SIMPLE, and always unclear. One was, why not take a bunch of old metal GRILLES to a welder, have him weld them together, and then put a big thick sheet of GLASS on top: a bedside table!

But John was a MINIMALIST! He didn't see why anybody needed a bedside table when you can put all your junk on the floor for FREE. John was INCENSED by Dot's purchases, the skittish egg cups, doilies, cracked plates and decoy ducks, that all seemed to need more DUSTING than they ever got. He had one personal possession – a fish fossil Dot had given him when they first met – and needed nothing more. John wanted a NICE CLEAN life, like the Ancient Egyptians! THEY never bothered with BEDSIDE TABLES. They lived off the flat of the land, saw everything from the side. Stripy tunics, beaded belts, skinny cattle, symmetrical legs, eye-liner, women with their breasts showing, men with erections, hieroglyphics all neatly stacked. John equated Nile with style.

Particularly perturbing to him was Dot's TEA-COSY COLLECTION. They reminded him of his grandma's UNDIES, saggy, baggy and stained (at some point she'd lost the knack of wiping her ass). They were not those stiff new William Morris monstrosities, padded semi-circles of artificial FIBRE that STORE well in DRAWERS (where such tea cosies BELONG). Dot's tea cosies were ancient home-made WOOLLEN concoctions, knitted by women inexplicably driven to provide the world with decorative structures in which to house teapots. Dot seemed to be one of the only people in England currently collecting tea cosies of this kind. Acquired fair and square from far-flung fêtes, or surreptitiously snatched from needless disuse in the kitchens of Jaywick Sands, Dot's collection would no doubt have

16

been FAMOUS if anyone CARED about tea cosies which they DON'T. You'd think, with pollution and over-population and the depletion of energy sources, retaining heat within a teapot would be given the respect it deserves but NO, nobody gives a FUCK about tea cosies. They all act like they've never SEEN one, or it's a hat.

Dot's tea cosies were a ratty bunch, bedecked with pompoms and polyps lovingly embroidered by gnarled hands, as well as more recent additions such as breadcrumbs, tea and jam smears (Dot was scared to wash them in case they SHRANK). They were also an UNWIELDY bunch, resistant to being folded or put in a pile. They would spring out of drawers unbidden and very slowly make their way across the counter like guilt-ridden animals, always ending up in the BUTTER or on the floor. Her favourite tea cosy was supposed to look like a basket of flowers. It had knitted pansies or petunias on top, and a floppy brown wool strap hanging against its side: the wicker handle of the basket! But she loved the others too. All gave stalwart service (insulation of a temporary nature) and made any teapot look good. Or SOFT anyway.

Jaywick itself is a tea cosy! An anachronism, a thing held dear only by old ladies, a thing full of HOLES. It is the CUNT of East Anglia. It has stared blankly at the sea for MILLIONS OF YEARS, engulfed by it when the tide was high.

It is everything at the bottom of your handbag! Slivers of glass, shreds of paracetamol, an old dried-up daisy, crumbs, dust, a blunt pencil, Kleenex, a scrap of paper bearing three-quarters of a phone number, a bedraggled tampon half out of its wrapper, a penny, and the tiny key to some long-gone suitcase.

Jaywick.

THIS IS NO PLACE TO BE!

DOT IN THE KITCHEN

Many insects lead, if they only knew it, UNLIVEABLE LIVES. Lives so vulnerable, so beset with disaster and purposeless suffering, that they would COMMIT SUICIDE if they only grasped this for a moment. Why is it only PEOPLE (and lemmings?) that see the horror of existence and do something about it? The microscopic red spider running along the edge of Dot's plate, making for an exit it cannot find, knows nothing of the horror of existence. It's hard to imagine a thing this small existing AT ALL. It is BARELY DETECTABLE. It doesn't even know how SMALL it is. How does it ever manage to find its own kind and MATE and make MORE of these? How big are the babies? Is the female mean to the male? Can it spin a web and catch bugs? How big are the BUGS? It senses food, air, light, heat, movement, gravity, it can run or stay still, it has few enemies except ACCIDENT OF EVERY SORT. This is a life?

50,000 times its size (and 50,000 times its self-importance), Dot very gently entices it on to a bit of torn-off newspaper (tricky to have anything to DO with something this small without KILLING it!), and puts the newspaper out on the window-ledge, hoping it's an OUT-DOOR spider. But later she wonders if she WRECKED ITS LIFE. That spider might have been in a state of ECSTASY, having just discovered in the glob of marmalade on Dot's plate enough food to live on for a YEAR, and even get quite BIG. Then she comes along and 'SAVES' it. But how was she to know it liked marmalade? What do we know about ANYONE?

Dot was now yanking hunks of FENNEL apart, in anticipation of John's return from a fishing trip. Dot existed, a blot in the universe, and she was making Cream of Fennel Soup with Tapenade Croutons. Like all gourmands, Dot and her hubby used food as a substitute for sex. But maybe sex is a substitute for FOOD. Food is essential, sex a LUXURY. Why else would it be so easily SUPPLANTED by shopping, gardening, cooking or watching TV (all unconscious FOOD-GATHERING activities – you may *think* you're not accomplishing much by watching TV for nine hours but you're actually accumulating DATA that might some day help in the search for FOOD: like a leopard up a tree, you're gaining perspective)? NATURE is confused about the matter, messily combining defecatory organs with reproductive ones in what is surely the weirdest anatomical ECONOMY DRIVE in the universe. MUST we all be SHAT OUT into the world?

Dot located a singed blue, pink and green tea cosy, wholly abstract and geometrical except for a topknot of yarn like a tuft of hair, and stuffed the hot teapot into it. Then she dumped the old wooden breadboard, fennel-soaked (in Dot's opinion, DIRTY), into the bin. This is so WRONG. People do not understand that wood has self-cleaning properties! It's ALIVE (sort of). Otherwise it wouldn't have been used for all this important domestic stuff like breadboards, rolling-pins, salad bowls, wooden spoons (carved for us, incidentally, by TINY UNPAID CHILDREN), butchers' blocks, tables, chairs, walls, floors, HOUSES. People think everything's got to be PLASTIC or METAL or at least SHINY to be healthy but they're all going to DIE because they're losing their immunity to GERMS while the wood-users will live, LIVE, surrounded by wooden objects and their wood-using children will flourish as they have flourished for millions of years. Wood-users survived and bred while SAND-users and LEAF-users and FEATHER-users and SHIT-users and PLASTIC-users all fell by the wayside! WOOD. It's an evolutionary PROCESS. Get with it.

There was a slight draught coming through a gap between the window and window frame, above the kitchen sink. Dot tried to sort of BEND the window back into position. John never got around to jobs like this. He always had to have the right TOOLS for things: he couldn't scrub a pan without a brand-new steel-wool pad (which he could never FIND), couldn't glue a chair leg on without the right size CLAMP. For quite a while he'd been putting off some job or other for want of Needle Nose Pliers. Dot didn't even know what they WERE (she thought he'd said, NEED-TO-KNOW

21

pliers!). John always made a meal of such tasks. It wasn't laziness but EFFICIENCY – of a peculiarly debilitating kind. Dot's solution worked fine. The window now shut.

Another mossy plant flew off the rock garden outside. Dot and John spent a fortune on little green and grey plants that blew away. Their rock garden wanted to be just ROCK, and resisted all plans for it to nourish LIFE.

Every feeling in the world has already been felt, thought Dot as she struggled with her soup stock. Everyone the SAME. And yet, bodies so different, forever alien. Wrinkles on knuckles in the wrong places – weird to have those hands. Hair always foreign, not like yours. And noses. How to relate to someone with a very different sort of nose? NO nose like YOUR nose.

Dot had just read that blue-eyed people instinctively prefer other blue-eyed people, and she wanted to tell John (whose eyes were NOT blue). They liked talking over interesting news items in the evening, with a bottle of wine and a filo-pastry parcel or two. Bitching about botch-ups: the NHS, the trains, the sinking of the *Belgrano*, the separation of India from Pakistan. They studied their rock garden as they discussed the deficiencies of the world, sheltered and snug like two peas in a pod!

They didn't know they were only POSING as happy. They thought a bottle of wine, a rock garden and thee WERE the requirements of happiness. But happiness is not in a plant, a pea-pod, or a filo-pastry parcel. It's not in any PACKAGE.

For Dot, happiness was in John's chin when it rubbed hers raw, his tongue deep in her mouth. Or when he grabbed her cunt while he fucked her, or splashed his cum on to her belly where she would spread it around with her hand. She also appreciated his sense of smell. A wife so unsensual she had to be REMINDED to smell things! Without John, Dot would have smelled only SHIT, sweat, shampoo and newly mown grass. Without John, Dot would have missed out on a LOT of apples and roses. She liked HIS smell too (he smelled of CINNAMON).

So her soul cried out to him!

DOT IN THE DISTANCE,
SEEN FROM THE SIDE

When he first met Dot, John had thought her head was full of lofty things: the arts, fossils, botany, astronomy. Later he'd realised she didn't know much and she dreamt only of PIE. He knew this because he'd asked her once why she smacked her lips in the night, and she'd admitted to dreaming CONTINUALLY of pie. Not just FRUIT pie either. She liked all kinds of pie, even things bearing little relation to pie, like SAMOSAS. Just the word on a menu lured her: Steak & Kidney Pie, Pork Pie, Shepherd's Pie, Banana Cream Pie, Mississippi Mud Pie, PAELLA.

Dot had once dreamt the QUEEN was coming to Jaywick (fat chance) and wanted to meet DOT. Dot was waiting for her at the Jaywick Community Centre, but the Queen was held up by well-wishers cheering her through the streets of Jaywick. Dot got so hungry waiting for the Queen that she started eating some very messy PIZZA. Her hands were all TOMATOEY when the Queen finally arrived. To Dot's shame and dismay, she was seated very CLOSE to the Queen! *Undone by pizza pie.*

The world is not a unified and harmonious structure. From the baby's desertion of the womb to the clear demarcations between land and sea, night and day, oil and vinegar, chalk and cheese, inside and out, substances seek SEPARATION. For every pull towards union there's equal or greater pressure to DIVIDE, disperse, disentangle, disintegrate. You never fully merge with anyone, you never fully UNDERSTAND anyone, including yourself. You come out of nothing, come out *with* nothing. It would be insulting to MISREPRESENT this, to suggest there could ever be togetherness that made up for how lonely we are.

John told PORKY PIES. Gone for weeks at a time, he claimed to be SWORDFISHING on a 73-foot, 365-horsepower, continuously welded steel vessel capable of speeds of 12 knots. It left Clacton every few months loaded with 40 miles of 700-pound test monofilament line, thousands of hooks, 5 tons of bait fish, an ice machine that could make 3 tons of ice a day, radar, loran, single sideband, VHF, a weather-track satellite receiver, a water-purifying machine that forced salt water through a membrane at 800 pounds per square inch, a Givens auto-inflating life raft, 7 type-one life preservers, 6 Imperial Survival suits, a 406 megahertz Emergency Position Indicating Radio Beacon (EPIRB), a 121.5 megahertz EPIRB, vice grips, prybar, hammer, crescent wrenches, files, hacksaws, channel-lock pliers, bolt cutters, a ball peen hammer, a spare starter motor, cooling pump, alternator, hydraulic hoses and fittings, v-belts, jumper wires, fuses, balls of STRING, needle nose pliers, hose clamps, gasket material, nuts, bolts, screws, cogs, wheels, sheet metal, silicone rubber, plywood, screw gum, duct tape, lube oil, hydraulic oil, transmission oil and fuel filters. The diesel fuel for the turbo-charged diesel engine was held in two 2,000-gallon tanks beside the engine and two 1,750-gallon tanks at the stern. Another 1,650 gallons were lashed to the whaleback in 30 plastic drums. 2,000 gallons of fresh water were stored in two forepeak tanks and another 500 gallons in drums on deck. The boat stayed in Clacton harbour just long enough to sell its catch, do repairs, get supplies and find enough crew members, before setting off again for GREENLAND where the men on it RISKED THEIR LIVES so that we can eat swordfish.

But not John. He wasn't swordfishing! He was just off having AFFAIRS.

Each apparently the apple of his eye, if his first choice didn't come to anything someone else would do. John's desires weren't generated by specific women, they were a constant stream which found various eddies. Recently, he'd moved swiftly along after a rebuff, but he was too FAST – she wanted him after all! So now he had THREE on the go, each equally dependent on his devotion and convinced of his FIDELITY, each apparently the apple of his eye.

Keeping all these women happy was an impossibility. In fact it gave him an excuse to keep NO woman wholly happy. They got their fractions of the pie. With his time scattered between women, work, wife, even DOGS IN THE STREET, John had reached the stage when he couldn't caress a breast without his loyalties being divided.

His real job was as a Careers Adviser for schools in Clacton and the surrounding area. This was mainly a matter of administering QUESTIONNAIRES. The kid would arrive in John's office, John would administer his questionnaire, analyse the results, and then almost invariably advise the kid to become a DENTAL PSYCHOLOGIST (somebody who holds people's hands at the dentist's) or some such job the kid had never heard of. It's precisely BECAUSE no one's heard of them that there are vacancies in these professions! Anyway, John was tired of directing people into computer jobs, call centres, and the Royal Marines.

INSATIABLE, his new woman's need for love, sex, food, booze. She threatens to call it off, saying that despite his charms and her love for him, she fears he will never be able to appease her neediness!

SOLUTION: John sits her down, says he won't leave her side until she asks him to. He stays with her, stares at her, holds her, talks to her, follows her into the loo, fondles her in bed all night, never letting her not feel his touch, his presence. When she's sick of the sight of him he goes out and returns with bags brimming. He cooks and cooks and makes her eat and eat until she refuses to eat any more! Still he makes her eat though. When she's full and fat he goes out again and returns with a litre of GIN and makes her martinis, very dry, day and night! She becomes aggressive after two but he keeps making them until she learns to drink four at a time without passing out. On waking he makes her more and when she is drunk and floppy he fucks her for hours. When he

27

gets tired he fucks her with a dildo, for hours and hours and hours. She becomes CONTENTED.

He was splendid in his way.

Like many morally uncertain men, John was always telling women what to DO. He was very free with his advice. There's nothing quite like an itinerant lover standing in your living room telling you to CALL YOUR FATHER or deal with your CHILD. He was always ready to propose some good deed to which his women could devote their lonesome weekends or dwindling cash reserves. He was a useful addition to any household! Well, an addition anyway.

One of his girlfriends landed a MODELLING job. She had been putting out the rubbish in her underwear (the bin was just a few feet from her front door), when she was SPOTTED by an advertising scout. They wanted her to model that season's underwear, in fact they were going to slap her whole BODY across the Eiffel Tower!

John was appalled. He'd left her a failed art history student, and come back to find her a STAR, thanks to RUNNING AROUND NAKED IN THE STREET. He berated her but she just giggled, and John had to acknowledge defeat – what man can compete with the EIFFEL TOWER?

He got home a little late that day, full of exciting news. 'I had to shake him to wake him up,' he recited with animation, recalling a heroic moment in the wheelhouse. 'He was sleeping at the WHEEL! I had to grab it and change course quick to avoid a collision. That bloke's been sacked. How's the wine?'

He poured himself a glass. Dot was at that stage of drunkenness when you think putting on your lipstick is EASY.

'Have to be off early tomorrow,' said John. 'We have to sharpen all the hooks, test the beeper buoys, adjust the crimper, make six thousand leaders and some ball drops, add three miles of mainline to the spool, service the air-pressure system, charge the salt water ice machine's compressor with Freon . . .'

It was sometimes an uphill struggle getting Dot interested in the workings of a swordfish boat (she was easily bored by sea breezes blowing at 15 knots, and responded best to accounts of John SAVING LIVES). But later they ate Cream of Fennel Soup (an aphrodisiac) with Tapenade Croutons (not so much) and were content.

What's it like to be named 'John' anyway? To be for ever one amongst so many. What does it say about your PARENTS? Did they find you boring FROM BIRTH? Or did they just want you to fit in with the crowd? (Why is THAT a good thing?) Does it give you HUMILITY to be named 'John'? Are you always sure your friends know WHICH 'John' they're talking to? (John got most of his girlfriends to call him 'Jack'.)

DOT IN POMPEII

Dot and John went to Naples! They fucked in the morning in front of the big mirrors on the wardrobe in their hotel room, then presented themselves downstairs for breakfast. It was a serve-yourself affair, with tiny rolls, white butter, ham, jam, fruit juice, and coffee that was not hot. A French woman complained in poor Italian that there was no CHEESE. There is so little assent in the world on the subject of breakfast.

Even Dot noticed the smell of orange blossom in the hotel garden, where lizards scampered over rocks. It was the first time she'd seen the Mediterranean!

They studied traffic interaction from their hotel window, which looked out on to a busy T-junction. Everyone seemed to have an equal right-of-way: scooters, buses, trucks and cars swerved round each other, honking but miraculously not hitting! Every once in a while a pedestrian would very slowly walk across the road. If you walked ELEGANTLY enough, you were safe. Hesitate – or RUSH it – and you're doomed.

They took a boat to Capri, saw the Blue Grotto, swam a mile off-shore, fell entwined upon a beach and lay there until waves measured their bulk. Then John ate a bad clam. So Dot went alone the next day to a shoe market and got lonely and depressed and chatted up, but managed to buy some nice shoes also.

They went by train to Pompeii. Dot had never believed that Pompeii really exists, BUT IT DOES. John bought a guide-book and read aloud to Dot about volcanic plugs and peristyles as they walked along. He told her Pompeii was dedicated to Venus, goddess of love and the regenerative force of nature. Her cunt still soft and sore from all their fucking, Dot approved of such forces. John ran off to check out the brothel with its two-thousand-year-old stone beds. They agreed to meet up in an hour at the amphitheatre.

There are many dots in Pompeii (two just in the NAME). Mosaics are made up of dots. The mouths and eye sockets of the corpses. The sun-glasses of the tourists and their camera lenses and the sausage slices on their pizzas and the chewing-gum they spit out on the ancient grooved roads. Tourists themselves are dots from a distance.

Dot could see them below her as she walked along the perimeter path on top of the city wall. She was all alone up there, with some faint sunshine hitting her right arm and a nice view of the mountains beyond. She thought of the doomed inhabitants of Pompeii who had seen the same view, and wondered yet again WHY they all died. Dot couldn't figure it out! They had died running, or crouched inside buildings, suffocating from fumes? Or ash?

Dot couldn't help wanting to give everybody a fairer chance of escape.

Dot's feet in their brand-new high-heeled sandals were beginning to HURT, blisters were forming, disaster loomed. But she soldiered on. Looking down at the ground, she noticed ANTS scuttling there beneath her thudding feet. POMPEIIAN ANTS, just going about their business, making plans, ENJOYING THEMSELVES, unaware that they were about to be OBLITERATED by some senseless, meaningless force (Dot). She TRIED to avoid stepping on them, but she was due in the amphitheatre!

You go to these historic places and you think you will be IMMUNE, that you can see and absorb historic places and historic CATASTROPHES and be unaffected. But Dot had seen how easily people can be obliterated, even people with GREAT INTERIOR-DECOR IDEAS, and it changed her. (She told John later but it didn't change him so MUCH.)

DOT IN DANGER!

On the eve of her fortieth birthday, Dot began to fear death. Up until then everything had been PERFECT. She had a perfect husband, perfect children (or WOULD have, if she'd ever had any), a perfect home, perfect body, perfect accoutrements, perfect table manners, a PERFECT LIFE! She even had friends in the Jaywick area with whom she played cards and WON. There was no other word for Dot and her life but: PERFECT.

Ah, but *near*-perfection's better! The haphazard, the untried. There's no FUTURE in perfection, nowhere left to go. There's no LIFE in it. You stop loving, stop trying, when everything is perfect.

There is pleasure in decay, in the awkward and the fumbling, a good pianist muffing a Schubert sonata. There is pleasure in states of disrepair, disuse, the doomed, degenerate, unconnected, out-of-place, the miserable, malodorous, uncorrected and uncontained. There is deep pleasure to be had in old cement and gravel, cemeteries and the overgrown gardens of people who don't care. In lakes the colour of anti-freeze, in which bacteria bloom. In rotting refuse and its attendant gulls, old army bases, abandoned runways, brickwork as it crumbles. Buddleia thrusting itself between forgotten railway sleepers – the smell of it is GREAT.

INDUSTRIAL WASTELAND, the last real wilderness on offer! Stare at the cracks in which green things grow.

At midnight on the dot, on the eve of her fortieth birthday, in perfect cliché fashion, Dot realised she would some day die. No amount of dieting, exercising, moisturising or medicating could avert it. Nor would MONEY help. Death would come, it was already on the way to her DOOR, and nobody could save her (nobody saved Schubert!). An unspeakably UGLY thing would come – death – uninvited and probably unannounced – to her – PERSONALLY – *some time* – and it would insist on being faced ALONE.

She might die AT ANY MOMENT. Dot lay in bed next to her magnificent hubby and thought she could already smell the putrefaction of her CORPSE. There was a slight whiff of it. Lying in bed on the eve of her fortieth birthday, Dot got a glimpse of her own SKELETON. She imagined herself just BONES: no skin, no fat, no muscle, no sinews, no tissues, no veins, arteries or capillaries, no eyes, no tongue, no ears, no glands, no valves, no membranes, no ducts, no enzymes, no bile, no saliva, NO NUTTIN. None of the glue that holds you together! Her skeleton, just LYING AROUND somewhere, long after her perfect tits and ass had MELTED AWAY, or been eaten by LARVAE or something, forgotten, all memory of her gone. Dot lay in bed on the eve of her fortieth birthday and realised that DEATH WRECKS EVERY-THING.

She listened to her breathing and thought, it might stop at any moment. One day it definitely WILL stop and that will be that. Unimaginable not to breathe! She grasped her rib-cage, felt her heart beating and knew that it could, and WOULD, one day stop, probably WITHOUT WARNING. No apology, no refund, NOTHING.

It could happen TONIGHT, thought Dot. And even if it doesn't happen tonight IT WILL HAPPEN. It will all be taken away from me, only hair and FINGERNAILS left, still GROWING. What is it with fingernails anyway? What do they think they're DOING? They think there's still HOPE? Do they expect to be RESCUED? Fingernails are CREEPY. They're actually little WIN-DOWS to the insides of your fingers! WHO NEEDS THIS?

On the eve of her fortieth birthday Dot finally managed to get to sleep. She dreamt about a kelim-clad alligator which had invaded her hotel room in some sunny clime. Dot did not think the hotel management would want an alligator in her room, so she tried to shoo it out on to the balcony. End of dream. The alligator probably represented Dot's grandmother but to explain why we'd have to go WAY BACK and that would cost you more (it would also negate the illusion of progress created by moving in a more or less forward direction).

Full of mortality fears and the alligator dream, Dot got up the next day – her BIRTHDAY! – and went to the kitchen to make John the perfect cup of tea. He always said it was perfect so she always tried to make it perfect again (he tried to ignore the crucial role TEA COSIES played in this process). John drank his first cup of tea in bed, which indeed IS the perfect way to start the day.

The day they were starting was starting elsewhere for six billion people, twenty billion chickens and fifty-four billion galaxies. Dot was just a dot in the COSMOS! Nonetheless, she was starting her day, as one must. I think toast and jam are called for, but opinions differ. I have had to eat SALAD on occasion, or cold soup, and once, THE TINIEST BAGEL IN THE WORLD.

Dot looked out of her kitchen window at her rock garden, what was left of it, and thought, I could die of cancer or a stroke. I could have a heart attack or liver failure or an EMBOLISM, or some long humiliating illness involving DIARRHOEA. I could die in a car crash, train crash, plane crash or ferry DISASTER. I could be MURDERED: stabbed, strangled, shot, garrotted, macheted, pulverised, electrocuted, torn LIMB from LIMB. I could die from neglect, exposure, sunstroke, malnutrition. I could be eaten by a SHARK (Dot had been badly affected by *Jaws*) or sputter out like the woman painted gold from head to toe in *Goldfinger* (likewise). I could be pelted with PUMICE STONES (Pompeii).

Dot realised she could die from her own mistakes or someone else's: she could walk out in front of a bus, eat something poisonous or place herself in the hands of a CRAZED ANAESTHESIOLOGIST. She could die EMBARRASSINGLY, drowning in a cup of coffee or having something silly fall on her head, like a poodle or pork chop, leading to a death no one can speak of without GIGGLING.

You can die having done everything right: Dot would die having completed any number of rearrangements of knick-knacks, and never having smoked a CIGA-RETTE. She would probably die before she'd sorted out her shoe rack or made much headway with the dried fruit she kept buying. You can die HEROICALLY, in some frantic aquatic rescue operation, or HAPHAZ-ARDLY, taking others with you: fire, flood, salmonella. At ANY MOMENT you could find yourself so ill you have to decide whether life is still worth LIVING, before it's TOO LATE and you're lying paralysed from the neck down in some hospital bed, having already watched all the *Columbo* episodes in the WORLD. Humbling, to have to lie there re-watching *Columbo*.

Dot could die before she was READY, in the middle of something she REALLY WANTED TO DO. Most of all, she didn't want one of those long lingering painful shameful deaths, with months of involuntary spasms, the colostomy bag, amputations, swollen MOON face, night-nurse brutality and other patients stealing from her purse. Dot craved and expected PERFECTION. Terrible trick to play on you if life were to end before you got it RIGHT.

After John left for work, Dot busied herself sweeping up the curled dead or dying wasps that lay about the hallway, lured there by the light she left on at night. DAYLIGHT had not cured her fears of mortality, so she resorted to HOUSEWORK.

But death's the best housekeeper! Does your dusting AND your polishing, eats the skin right off your BONES.

And so began the traumatic year of 1996.

THE TRAUMATIC YEAR OF 1996

Dot in the universe. No more or less significant than anyone else. Nor was she perfect. She THOUGHT she was, apart from her Fatal Flaw. This was a bit like a third nipple or birthmark you can't get rid of (though it was neither of these). Trust me, modern medicine offered no solution, nor was the problem covered in the Trusty Tips section of *The Clacton Wanderer* (serving Clacton and the surrounding community).

Apart from that Fatal Flaw though, Dot considered herself pretty sweet and nice! And it was her intention only to become SWEETER and NICER. Poor duck, she believed that niceness could grow! She had failed, despite forty years of existence, to note the universality of decay.

When the weather cleared at 3:30, nice sweet Dot set off for the shops. The roads, though muddy, were not busy. 3:30 is not RUSH HOUR in Jaywick Sands. Dot reached the corner shop without incident.

The corner shop wasn't actually on a corner, nor was

it close to Dot's house. So when she mentioned 'the corner shop', people often thought she meant ANOTHER shop that WAS on the corner. But that shop was hardly ever OPEN and was hardly what you'd call a SHOP. The one Dot called 'the corner shop' was much more like a typical corner shop than the real corner shop would ever be.

A window ran the length of the shop-front, displaying old fruit in separate boxes. Sometimes a box was getting kind of low, the apples wrinkled and dented and the oranges mouldy. Bananas hung above, sometimes greenish, sometimes just right, but more often speckled and bruised. People have never reached AGREEMENT on ripeness in a banana. This is what makes selling bananas such a FREE-FOR-ALL.

High above were things that nobody understood or bought, though they might have if they'd known they were there: hair grips, combs, toothbrushes, beach toys. Below, in darkness, lurked vegetables. Vacuum-packed into the rest of the shop were all the other necessities for a MINIMAL LIFE in Jaywick. The shop wasn't MESSY, it was just stuffed to the BRIM. Old ladies came in who didn't want to search for anything, so the shopkeeper man or woman would come out from behind the counter to help them. They also emerged to get you your fruit (in case you dented it MORE) and the (invisible) vegetables.

Dot and John had a funny story about the shopkeeper couple which they told at dinner parties. John's car had broken down once in a country lane and he needed to phone the AA. So he knocked on the door of a nearby farmhouse, and who should poke their heads out of the upstairs window but the shopkeeper couple? In their JAMBOS. Dot and John had always assumed they lived above (or below) the SHOP, but in fact they merely exploited Jaywick all day and ESCAPED it at night! (Good idea.)

Dot was in a hurry. She only wanted to buy a few dull items here before driving on to the Safeway's in Clacton. As she entered the shop she gave an old lady by the door quite a BUMP. Dot felt bad about this and made apologetic manoeuvres to get around the woman, while secretly hoping the mishap would enable her to beat the old bird to the TILL!

Women when shopping are DIFFERENT, not so nice. You see them in supermarkets, eyeing their prey. It is the primitive life of the hunter-gatherer. She seeks. She listens to stirrings in the forest (of aisles), her eyes attuned to any sign of a bargain. She is not bedazzled by plumage and packaging. Nor does she feel the cold as she nears the refrigerated section. FOOD ON THE TABLE: that is her quest.

Dot rushed around finding things and was standing innocently in line near the till, safe in the belief that she would soon be served, when she heard a crash. By squidging too close to the woman in front in order to gain a firm place in the notional queue, Dot had managed to knock over an entire stack of NOODLES, on Special Offer. Dot now had to give up her promising position in the queue in order to RE-ERECT the stack of noodles. There proved to be a KNACK to stacking that Dot LACKED. Every time she got the goddam

41

noodles into a pile they fell down again, tubes, bows, shells, stars, dots, space-ships, the LOT. When Dot looked up from her stacking she found the queue had become impossibly long, and her RIVAL was in it!

Dot suddenly gave up on EVERYTHING, maybe even life itself. She no longer saw the POINT of noodles – why do people need their food curled, tied or TWISTED into silly shapes? What does this say about HUMANITY? Dot could not resurrect the stack of noodles, she couldn't beat the old biddy, had no TIME for this nonsense anyway, needed to LEAVE. So in the end she just sort of TIDIED the bags of noodles on the floor, gave the woman shop-keeper a look meant to seem abashed but received as surly, and left the shop feeling quite flustered. She didn't under-stand why people had to be so UNPLEASANT when she tried so hard to be NICE.

Brooding on this and whether John would prefer her birthday supper to be Stir-fried Squid with Chilli, Chorizo, Tomatoes, Baby New Potatoes and Roasted Red Peppers OR Sea Bass with Salsa Verde on a bed of Wild Mushroom Risotto (Rick Stein has a lot to answer for), Dot drove rather hastily up Lincoln Convertible Avenue to Buick, then on to Daimler. She crossed Volvo with the intention of reaching Range Rover the back way via Humber, and was just speeding up as she neared the edge of town when she noticed roadworks at the junction of Vauxhall Terrace and Cuttlefish Crescent, a tricky spot (all those TENTACLES). Not wishing to SLOW DOWN (it being her custom when leaving Jaywick to make a quick getaway), Dot skilfully mounted the bank where a child was playing and ZIPPED past a big road-work machine that was scooping stuff. She was momentarily absorbed by the grace and skill with which the scooper was scooping and distracted enough by this to hit what she thought was a traffic cone. She pressed on, gripping the steering wheel with tense and scrawny hands.

But there was something funny about hitting that cone, something UNFORGETTABLE. Once you've hit one you've got to hit ANOTHER. She sent several spinning, and watched them hopping about in her rear-view mirror as she raced through the countryside looking for MORE CONES. In her exhilaration she nearly hit a dog, a cat, a man in an electric wheelchair, a mouse and a magpie. She did run over some bugs (who KNOWS how many?) but nothing stopped her until she reached her favourite parking place at Safeway's in Clacton (serving Clacton and the surrounding area). THEN she remembered the Sea Bass, the Risotto, and the KID – was there really a kid? – and vomited out the door into her favourite parking place (needless to say, her favourite parking place no longer).

To sum up. Dot left the house that afternoon feeling SWEET and VULNERABLE, a Birthday Girl! She returned some hours later a malevolent MONSTER, a femur-smashing FEMME FATALE whose Fatal Flaw was now the least of her worries. The repercussions of the car crash were numerous and complex and would need to be looked at by an EXPERT. I will elucidate but a few.

One repercussion was that Dot no longer felt she was a GOOD DRIVER! She consequently became a slightly

WORSE driver, and drove with no ENJOYMENT, aware that elation can get the better of you and one thing lead to another until there are CONES flying and CREATURES DYING all over the godforsaken east coast of ENGLAND.

Another repercussion was the expense of getting a new car (Dot had a PHOBIA about the old one) and dealing with the new car mechanic in his bright-yellow overalls, who liked to explain car-engine intricacies in DETAIL. There were also insurance forms to fill out and legal letters that Dot was supposed to OPEN and READ.

Then there were all the radio bulletins about the boy's progress (he'd broken his leg), followed eventually by frightened visits by Dot to the HOSPITAL to see the boy and his mother, who was very ANGRY. Also, whenever crashes or boys or cones were mentioned on TV, Dot felt faint.

Going places was complicated by Dot's determination to avoid the crash SITE and anything associated with the crash (the corner shop and Cuttlefish Crescent were both ruled out). As a result Dot's CARD GAME suffered. She didn't even go to the ALTERNATIVE corner shop any more because she'd once seen someone going in who LOOKED like the boy's mother and just the POSSI-BILITY that it MIGHT be the mother was enough to send Dot home in a tremble.

Dot was appalled by the woman's FURY. People act like there's some intrinsic MERIT in motherhood and the way mothers behave. But every LIZARD thinks well of its offspring! Swans go to infinite pains for theirs. What

44

does THAT prove? Fish sensibly ignore the whole business. Salmon have a purely romantic view of procreation – just an all-out battle upstream for the fuck of a lifetime and then TO HELL WITH IT.

Dot's nerves were SHOT. John heard one day that some friends of theirs had had a baby. He and Dot went straight out to buy something celebratory for dinner. They got lamb chops. These reduced in the cooking, giving off a large amount of GREASE. Dot picked at what looked like two little kidneys on her chop. They made her think of the NEW BABY'S KIDNEYS. She began to feel like she was EATING THE BABY. She told John they were eating the baby and they both looked disgustedly at their plates. Dot's chop still lay there but John's was GONE, he'd EATEN it already. Dot made do with apple pie for supper that night.

Now, if Dot had been a heroic housewife in an American TV movie (a saxophone playing incessantly in the background), she would have rehabilitated herself through GOOD WORKS, befriended the boy, later SAVED HIS LIFE somehow, and become BOSOM PALS with his mother (who wasn't angry after all, just needed a FRIEND). Dot would later have spearheaded the national campaign against traffic-cone derangement, ending up on Capitol Hill tearfully recalling how she had fought her own addiction to the accursed things: 'Traffic cones were my undoing, especially those nice *yellow* ones . . .'

But Dot WASN'T in a movie (she just thought she was sometimes). In the absence of a clear and noble MISSION, she cleaned cabinets with a dubious sponge, attempted

NONCHALANCE, and longed quite often for easeful death.

Thoughts of interior decoration were her only consolation – decor, like matter, can never really be created or destroyed. But there is an element of MEGALOMANIA in knowing exactly how a place should look. Dot wanted "Oceania" to look more like the house in which she'd grown up. To achieve this, she needed a PALE-YELLOW BATHROOM. But Belinda Lurcher was always warning people that yellow is a difficult colour to get right. This threw Dot into DECOR DOUBT.

Another problem arose concerning a wallpapering table. On hearing that Dot was redecorating, some friends offered her their wallpapering table. Dot thought they were GIVING it to her. Later, the husband called up and complained to John about the NON-RETURN of the table. Dot called back and got the wife. Dot said she would be HAPPY to return the wallpapering table. The wife said, 'What would WE do with it?' So Dot kept the table.

Some time later the couple called again to say they wanted their wallpapering table BACK, or else they wanted Dot to PAY for it. Dot did then offer to buy the fucking table. The hubby's response was to ask Dot what she wanted for CHRISTMAS. Dot said what she wanted was to be allowed to BUY THE TABLE. It was all a big misunderstanding (I STILL don't understand it).

To make up for it all, the couple asked Dot and John out to see their new country cottage, so off Dot and John went into unknown reaches of Essex. When they arrived, the wifey was on the PHONE, and

REMAINED on the phone for half an hour. Then she said she had to MOW THE LAWN (gardening's another form of megalomania). When you finally FIND somebody's country cottage you expect to be greeted, if not amply FED. FUCK THE LAWN, Dot was HUNGRY. When they did sit down to eat, they were SURROUNDED by the smell of newly mown grass. This is actually a MASSACRE-ALERT smell. It is the smell given off by injured blades of grass in an attempt to WARN OTHERS. It is the smell of grass in a PANIC – there's nothing NICE about it.

DUMPING THE BODY

Pears hang heavy in October. Leaves were moving along the ground in a way they have that seems to MEAN something.

Dot's hands were cold. They were ALWAYS cold in Jaywick. She was sick of it. She was sick of the SEA, its ceaseless MOVEMENT. What do FISH make of it? How can they BEAR it? You get TIRED of that sort of thing after a while.

Dot was loading the last of the stuff she needed to take to the dump. To a casual observer it might have looked like she was having a big Spring Clean! But Dot was expelling her whole EXISTENCE. As she drove out of Jaywick past fat-assed women on sofas watching Julia Roberts movies in the afternoon, the sky was a deep bright blue.

Tiny despots in a universe that may be equally despicable. Meaningless, ourselves and all about us. And running the whole show, something just as random, accident-prone and undesirable, with uncertainty built into its FOUNDATIONS. The universe! Unlikely but possible that we and it could disappear at any time.

Abjectly terrified of death, Dot had decided to CONTROL it – by committing suicide. But she wanted to do it RIGHT, make all the necessary PREPARATIONS. So she had cooked up several gourmet meals and stuck them in the freezer for John to heat up after her demise. She had also made enough raspberry jam to last him a YEAR.*

She had tidied the house until it SPARKLED, even the kitchen DRAWER. Before Dot tidied it the drawer had: two fruit-inlaid lollipops from long ago (one lime, one pineapple), half a packet of cut-flower food, an old library card, the stamp book, an address stamp ("Oceania", 11 Abalone Avenue, Jaywick Sands, Nr. Clacton, ESSEX CO4 3BQ) and accompanying ink-pad, pens, pencils, scissors, a key-ring, a tape measure, beads, Band-Aids, vitamins, masking tape, a Chinese take-away menu, paperclips, batteries (old and new), fuses (ditto), an egg-timer, rubber bands, a tiny miniature bottle of Tabasco Sauce (half-empty), Swan matches, a free sample packet of cough lozenges, chewing-gum, a small knitted COW, a faulty pocket-watch Dot had given John on their tenth anniversary, shells, sand, raffle tickets, playing cards, chess pieces, cocktail umbrellas, three chopsticks, a tiny wooden doll's

* Dot's recipe for Raspberry Jam (we might as well MAKE USE of her while we still can): Put 1 lb raspberries and 1 lb sugar in a pan and leave overnight. Next day, bring this to the boil and continue cooking for about 4 MINUTES, until it reaches the Soft Ball Stage. Pour into heated jars and cool.

49

house TELEPHONE, a paper poppy from Remembrance Day, a toy Easter chick with real feathers dyed bright yellow and plastic feet, out-of-date coupons and a dry shrivelled apple core. AFTER she cleaned it, the drawer contained: two pens, two pencils, a pair of scissors, the stamp book, the address stamp and ink-pad, and the masking tape. She'd tidied all the LIFE out of it!

Having phoned several craft museums, Dot gave up hope of finding an appreciative home for her tea-cosy collection. She had never realised before just how indifferent to tea cosies the nation was! Unable herself to throw them away, this was one task she would have to leave to John.

She had thought of donating some money to charity before she died. You couldn't walk down Clacton High Street without someone yelling 'BRAIN-DEAD CHILDREN' at you, or 'BEDSORES'. But she had been unable to find a charity specifically devoted to the MIDDLE-AGED (unless you count the National Trust). She gave her best duds to Oxfam and left it at that.

She had written John a GOODBYE CARD. Her clean-lined, clean-living hubby – every angle of him was straight, if you saw him from the back or the side or the front! His thin lips and closely clipped hair and somewhat stern manner: he was unbending, unwrinkled, IRONED-OUT, and surprisingly resistant to the weather at sea. In her note, Dot said she was sorry to miss out on time with him but it was for the best and she loved him LOADS. (Look, it was a SUICIDE NOTE, it was bound to be inadequate.)

Dot's effects seemed to have little effect on the dump. There was a peculiar LIFE to the place that Dot didn't like. People throw a lot of things away, not just TRASH but nice hat boxes and frilled dressing tables, velvet curtains and upholstered furniture, suitcases, clothing, crockery. It all sits at the dump and rots, and it's COLOURFUL. Dot noticed an empty jar of Enchilada Sauce, half a cardboard jewellery box, the lid from a take-away coffee. A delicate pink plastic carrier bag was drifting along in the wind.

Places left to rot become THEMSELVES. Like a body, some bits untended – the cheesy belly button, cracked heels, dirty ass. There is beauty in decay.

On her return home from the dump, Dot propped her suicide note up on the mantelpiece in the living room, fashioned a noose out of her imitation-basket tea cosy and, slipping the handle of it round her neck, kicked away the kitchen chair and started to die.

To die in Jaywick!

But the rattiness of Dot's tea cosies was her SALVA-TION. Despite all the engineering know-how that had gone into its making, the criss-cross basketry pattern and all the superfluous leaves and pansies on the top (or perhaps BECAUSE of them), the basket tea cosy had been OVER-USED, and though frail, petite, slight, feminine, perfect (almost) and an EMBLEM OF HER ERA, Dot was too heavy for her own tea cosy! It began to tragically unravel and then to SPLIT in fibrous ways. Dot fell, unconscious, to the floor.

When John strolled in on this scene, his wife like

SNOW WHITE beside what appeared to be the woolly remains of some savage RODENT, he called the police. They came, inspected Dot, called in a GP to certify her dead, and took her off to the morgue (serving Clacton and surrounding area). People are ALWAYS DOING THIS. They are always declaring middle-aged women dead when they're NOT!

Dot was tucked neatly into a drawer for the night, all cosy-like, and was about to be rolled into OBLIVION, when the policeman who'd brought her in noticed her big TOE was moving. He gingerly prodded her shoulder. Dot sat up and started tugging at the name-tag on her toe, which itched. The policeman gave her a cup of tea, and himself one too – he'd had quite a shock.

Later, he told reporters from *The Clacton Wanderer*, 'It's your worst nightmare: instead of being dead you're alive!'

DOT ON TRIAL

When her Reckless Driving case came to court, Dot wore: a nice grey suit (tight skirt and fitted jacket), taupe shoes and a matching handbag. She did not see how she could be CONVICTED in such a smart outfit, and she was RIGHT: everyone in the room was CHARMED by Dot's outfit.

Having sat through many TV courtroom dramas, Dot knew it would be futile and tedious not to tell the truth. She even volunteered information about the CONES.

'So, you did not knowingly leave the scene of the accident. You were unaware of there having BEEN an accident, is that correct?' asked the solicitor acting for the little boy.

'Yes,' said Dot, a glory in grey.

'You did not see the boy?'

'No.'

'Did you not notice that you had hit something?'

'Oh, yes, but I thought it was a traffic cone,' said Dot, smoothing her skirt.

'A traffic cone!?'

'Yes. I thought I'd hit a traffic cone.'

'So what did you do then?'

'I looked for more traffic cones to hit!'

Laughter and cheers from the public benches.

'I hope you are not trying to be FUNNY, Mrs Butser.'

'No, m'lord.'

'Because that would be a much more serious offence.'

Despite a bit of kerfuffle from the boy's mother, who ran at Dot and tried to pull her hair after the acquittal, everyone else seemed to understand that Dot had suffered enough. Accidents happen. And she had that nice grey SUIT. They understood that her mind had been on other things (suicide and Sea Bass) and they forgave her!

Fortified by this success, as well as a coquettish flirtation with her solicitor, Dot went on to take action against the GP who had certified her dead when she was NOT dead. The policeman who'd saved her came and testified on her behalf in a pale-blue suit that matched his eyes. Dot got £38,000 COMPENSATION! John hadn't expected her to get ANYTHING. No one knows exactly what value to put on human life.

Full of a newfound optimism, Dot went straight to her favourite junk shop and bought a FRENCH BENCH. (She had long envied her neighbour's garden seat.)

A TASTE FOR BLOOD

Dot had been infuriating other women all her life, she was so PERFECT. But she WASN'T that great really. Another repercussion of the car crash I forgot to mention was that Dot developed a taste for BLOOD. Ever since she'd crashed into that kid she had had fantasies about crashing into MORE people. She knew it was pretty unlikely she'd get away with more than one hit-and-run (even in that suit), so she turned her homicidal thoughts to the systematic dispatch of OLD LADIES, like the one who'd been in her way that fateful day at the corner shop.

Old ladies are ALWAYS in the way! IRRITATING OLD LADIES with their frumpish rumps, requiring deference and patience as they waddle in front of you or dither and stop dead in their tracks for NO GOOD REASON. They really take it out of you! Somehow you are always exerting yourself for old ladies, and always at the WORST TIME. Dot had been dutifully tending old ladies for years, not just the ones near by and not just

NICE ones either but cranky, obstreperous, malevolent old ladies all over Jaywick and the surrounding area, UNKIND old ladies good at getting what they want and full of suspicion and CONTEMPT for Dot because she was young, pretty, blonde and (apparently) PERFECT. Dot hated them too and was sick of listening to them complain about the weather or the Royals or the price of LARD. Old ladies had already had the BEST of Dot. They'd bled her DRY. The law against murder is after all so arbitrary.

Jaywick turned out to be the ideal place to commit murder! Its rickety bungalows attracted vulnerable old ladies, husband-free, ripe for annihilation, the wind muffled their screams, and nobody gave a damn.

Long after they'd switched off their TV sets, glugged their last mouthfuls of Ovaltine (for ever), brought in their favourite gnomes from the garden and settled down for some peevish rest, Dot would creep in and set TRAPS for them. After one of Dot's nocturnal visits, an old lady got out of bed in the middle of the night and, tripping over her own gnome, landed heavily on an aerosol deodorant can neatly glued with undetectable flour-and-water paste to an upturned nail in the floor. The impact of her rump on the can caused it to puncture and burst into FLAMES (luckily the old lady died of shock before the fire took hold). The police considered it just another OLD-LADY MISHAP. Old ladies die by the DOZEN all over the world and nobody does a thing about it.

Dot was still visiting many old ladies for afternoon tea. She dealt with their toe-nails while they told her things. They were happy to tell her the SAME things each time, it didn't matter to THEM. But instead of being bored, Dot had a new purpose in life. She would cheerfully carry the tea tray back to the kitchen ('So helpful!'), steal the tea cosy, leave the gas on unlit, or fill the sugar bowl with carpet cleaner (a typical old-lady mistake), and smilingly depart. Within a week, another little obituary in *The Clacton Wanderer* and a FOR SALE sign rattling in the wind.

Dot was GOOD at this! She began to feel she had divine powers over life and death. They were dying like FLIES, the old ladies of Jaywick Sands.

Dot's next-door neighbour had long been a handful, always complaining about things and getting Dot to do her shopping or check the electricity meter to make sure the electricity company wasn't cheating her, or phone the council to find out when the next rubbish collection would be (she never believed the dustmen would stick to their appointed day). She also had a FROG PHOBIA. Dot was supposed to inspect the old bat's back garden frequently for frogs and REMOVE them if necessary. This was a big mistake, for it gave Dot an idea.

The next time Dot came across a frog migration point on the road to Wivenhoe, she disgustedly collected about thirty of them in a carrier bag. That night she set them free, emptying the bag into her neighbour's garden. When the old lady trundled outside the next day to water her marigolds, she noticed an odd-shaped stone. Bending over to get a closer look, she caught sight of TWO EYES staring back at her. Already overbalanced, she lost her footing, hit her head against the far end of the fish pond, yelped 'HELP!', and drowned.

It was like the anguished yelps of ANIMALS IN THE NIGHT. Animals too suffer from fear of death. They too must wonder, is this all my life is going to BE? Is this IT?

Dot thought old ladies were better off dead (MOST people think this), rather than dealing with the corner shop or the SEA, that terrible sea, full of creatures you want nothing to do with! They slept so deafly, so blindly, as Dot crept by their beds (their SEA BEDS), their bodies already FESTOONED with decay.

WHAT ABOUT THE BODY JUNK? The scars, the wrinkles, the stretchmarks, liver spots, polyps, the hopeless meaningless flab, the wonky tortoiseshell toe-nails and bags under the eyes like SCROTAL SACS, the weird bruises old ladies get, the furrowed brow and no sign of a neck at all? And that was just on the OUT-SIDE, where you put the stuff that can be left out in the rain. The more delicate antiques were INSIDE, piled HIGH, all higgledy-piggledy, a slapdash mishmash of organ failure, embolism, dyspepsia, diplopia and clogged synapses. THESE were the true junk shops of Jaywick Sands.

Time for the old HEAVE-HO!

DOT REBORN

We're held so tightly to the earth. It would have changed everything if humans could fly. You'd get some perspective. Pollution? Pah! Slaughterhouses? Fie! War? Too tiring. Dishonesty? NOT POSSIBLE.

If you looked at John's life from a distance, you'd see the wreckage all around him, how he'd sacrificed everything, wife, career, ideals, all sense of SECURITY, to sex, let everything go to POT for sex, like a foaming CAMEL or a crab. If you didn't KNOW about the affairs you'd still see signs of neglect all around the guy. He'd once had a SPARK. He always told himself he had affairs because his wife was dull, but in fact he'd failed to keep her INTERESTING, because it was so much easier having AFFAIRS.

Nor was he brave: Dot's suicidal weirdness had unnerved him. Like his mother after she had HIM, John felt inclined to desert a sinking ship.

John was hoping DOT would get some perspective if they drove all the way to Padstow to eat fish at Rick Stein's restaurant. They had wanted to eat fish at Rick Stein's restaurant for many years. They were even perhaps a little OVER-PREPARED for the experience of eating fish at Rick Stein's restaurant.

In the car, they gobbled huge bon-bons: Mint Humbugs. John always furnished the car with travel sweets for long journeys – he was a FUN KIND OF GUY. Unable to SPEAK because of all the humbugs, they played tapes of bluegrass music, John demonstrating his banjo-plucking technique on Dot's knee. His more complex plucking motions helped to distract Dot from his DRIVING, which otherwise made her nervous. A passing truck flicked a rock into the windshield, causing a small CRACK and making the trip feel ILL-OMENED, but it didn't stop them going to Padstow.

They spent a night in Lyme Regis on the way. The hotel had seen better days, as had the town, but they felt serene there, promenading on precipitous paths. The Channel looked much BLUER than the North Sea.

They went into a tiny café where impatient dogs were awaiting someone's return. On the wall were little PAINTINGS done on cigarette packets and other empty containers: flower compositions and other more whimsical stuff. They were for sale! Dot bought two, one of roses against a black background, the other a *trompe-l'oeil* ASHTRAY with a smoking cigarette in it, painted on an old Camembert box. They were PERFECT, Dot thought. But a life based on perfection is a charade, a fraud carried out on yourself. Accept this and you're in with a chance. Refuse and you get nothing.

Their hotel room had beautiful french windows that opened on to a shared balcony. It was warm out so they left the windows open all night. The next morning the hotel CAT came in off the balcony, jumped on the bed and kneaded John's buttocks, not unpleasurably, while John fucked Dot (no extra charge).

On reaching Padstow they headed straight for Rick Stein's restaurant, where they had some oysters and champagne! They had a nap at their guest house, followed by a stroll, and then RETURNED to Rick Stein's restaurant in the evening to eat *Pulpo a la Feria*, Isinglass Sorbet, Prawn Jambalaya, Crushed New Potatoes with Watercress, and starfish-shaped cookies for dessert with their coffee. Everything on the menu cost £400. There was no sign of Rick Stein himself – a great disappointment to Dot who had long yearned for him in his buttoned-up white chef's shirt.

The guest house was rudimentary, the breakfast bad, and there was no SEX CAT. As soon as they'd paid, they went straight to Rick Stein's BISTRO (a subsidiary of the restaurant) for an early lunch of Clappydoo Chowder, Mussel and Truffle Torte, Crayfish Gumbo, Monkfish and Turbot Timbale, and Crushed New Potatoes with Watercress on the side (£400). They told the waitress they were thinking of staying FOR EVER but that was just silly and a LIE: on exiting the restaurant they set off immediately for home.

Dot felt REBORN, particularly when John played banjo on her knee (there's an animality about music which is its hidden charm). But John had a surprise for Dot when they reached their house at 11 Abalone Avenue: his 'penpal', a bedraggled girl named Julie, whom Dot had never heard of before, was sitting on their doorstep. Dot obligingly made up a bed for her on the couch. She stayed for WEEKS.

Julie was a quiet girl. The only problem was the way she SMOKED: she flicked her cigarette ash in the DIRECTION of the ashtray, not IN. Julie even used the brand-new painted *trompe-l'oeil* ashtray AS AN ASH-TRAY and stubbed her cig OUT in it, unperturbed that the cig continued to burn, as well as the ashtray itself. Julie never noticed that it WAS a painted *trompe-l'oeil* imitation of an ashtray.

Julie came into the kitchen one morning when John was at work, and announced to Dot, 'I give good head. I fuck really good.'

Clutching a tea cosy like a SHIELD, Dot offered Julie some tea. Julie payed no attention.

'I'm quite famous in the business for double-penetration,' she told Dot. 'I'm willing to do anal if the guy's not too big.'

Julie had been a plain old 'Reader's Wife' in a porn mag in Birmingham before she was DISCOVERED and sent to London to fuck some guy in a MOVIE. She returned to Birmingham full of excitement about her new career. But her hubby seemed a little HUFFY: he'd wanted to SHOW HER OFF, not SHARE.

The marriage over, Julie had gone back to London to seek her fortune, and now lived in a flat in Shoreditch with nothing in it except a telephone and a pair of trainers – with the phone she received notification of future porn opportunities, with the shoes she could RUN AWAY from it all in the end. It was as if she had just INVENTED herself, just scrabbled out of an EGG.

Julie spoke of her body as a WORK TOOL only; she was always getting stuff stuck into it or SUCKED OUT (a great fan of liposuction). In fact she considered plastic surgery essential to her career and spent most of her porn income on getting it done. She'd had LOTS of different BREASTS. She talked about them like OPTIONAL EXTRAS – she just couldn't decide how big they ought to BE.

The last movie she'd made was a Gothic horror thing. They had to film it at night with a lot of fake FOG, to which Julie was ALLERGIC. They kept pumping the fog at her when she was supposed to be giving somebody a BLOW-JOB, and it made her COUGH. She ended up fucking up the FUCKING scene too with her coughing. That was when she'd decided to accept John's invitation to the seaside.

Julie had first met John on a PORN FILM SET, where his ability to maintain an erection was much in demand. 'If you're good at something, you should be proud of it,' Julie proclaimed.

When Dot confronted John about all this on his return that evening, he said he'd gone into porn merely to augment his meagre income so that he could take Dot to Padstow after her suicide attempt (Rick Stein has a lot to answer for); the affair with Julie was just an occupational hazard.

There is so much we accept as the NORM, so much stuff under the surface we don't look at because IT AIN'T PRETTY. The weirdness of desire, of fucking or NOT fucking the same person more than once, the wish to fuck AT ALL in between the eating and the shitting and the sleeping and the dreaming and the dressing and the undressing and all the DRIVING, this constant MOVE-MENT. Let's face it, we're all SICK AS DOGS most of the time.

So hard being alive, all the things you have to cope with, merely to exist: heat, cold, rain, pain, hunger, vomiting, defecation, menstruation ... No wonder ADULTERY is the last straw for some women. Dot went down to the junk shop and bought a big old white CHEESE DISH, big enough to put her SORE HEAD in. It was shaped like a STONE, with an encrustation of oak leaves on the top and shallow ridges down the side. Like a STONE it sat in the kitchen after she left (John didn't even LIKE cheese).

But what could he do? John was tired of lying, tired of carrying out a fraud on HIMSELF. Accept something and you're in with a chance, refuse and you get nothing. What John GOT with Julie was a pretty good *trompe-l'oeil* imitation of a marriage. The two little birch trees stood for John and Julie just as they had for John and Dot: forlornly.

DOT REBORN (AGAIN)

As from today, Dot Butser has changed her name to Dorothea de Radziwill Butser.

This is following on from the traumatic year of 1996 which she now wants to put behind her and start life anew.

Dorothea **is the name by which she was known before her marriage,** ***de*** **is a family name, and** ***Radziwill*** **is her maiden name.**

This distinguishes her from her ex-husband's mother and any possible future marriage of her ex-husband.

With the help again of her solicitous solicitor, Dot managed to hold on to all of the £38,000 compensation for being almost buried alive, and got a promise of receiving a portion of John's future income, from porn or any other source (pimping, prostitution, gambling, extortion, ETC). With this, her new name, and her tea cosies, Dorothea de Radziwill Butser set off on a new life!

But let's not DELUDE ourselves. Dot was not exactly 'reborn'. She was still the same old Dot, her body just a dot in the universe. INEVITABLE rather than brave, that she should go on tending it, with food and water, clothing and shelter, to her dying day. She was STUCK with it!

Enraged by the east, defeated by the south and west, Dot headed north to the oceanic landscape of Yorkshire between Accrington and Burnley. But how can you ever feel safe when geological eminences keep BULGING at you, ominously obscuring things, the countryside folding and unfolding itself before your eyes, turning itself INSIDE OUT and threatening to COLLAPSE at any moment? Dot didn't need this, land pretending to be water! Dot had had ENOUGH of the sea.

She moved on to Edinburgh, where she wound up in a B & B in Morningside run by an actor called Umberto Opignanesi. His acting consisted of tiny parts in Shakespeare, usually CARRYING a spear, but he wielded great power at home.

There were two bathrooms (shared), no apparent heat source, and lousy breakfasts (despite daily efforts, Mrs Opignanesi never mastered the EGG). Dot didn't speak to the people she shared a bathroom with, she just heard them on the stair, or saw them at breakfast where NO ONE could talk over the sound of the radio pumping out terrible pop music, rushed news reports and deafening ads.

Guests were supposed to be OUT most of the day. 'Out!' Mr Opignanesi would yell, threatening them all with his spear. So Dot wandered the streets of Edinburgh, EDINBURGH – with its cosmopolitan range of shops, discos and veterinarians, its Georgian terraces and medieval passageways, its dark cobble-stones (blue-grey when wet), its clouds and low-slung light, its drunks, its many hospitals, hostelries and hostilities, its women with nasty coughs but real wicker SHOPPING-BASKETS, its traffic dilemmas, dog shit, and the Water of Leith, which offers FORGETFULNESS.

Dot became a dot on the pavement, as anonymous as any man in the street.

THE MAN IN THE STREET

There are many men in the street. MOST men make it out on to the street at some point. You see them walking along there. For YOU they are just part of the STREET. You forget they have HOMES, friends, desks, piles of PAPER. It is impossible to conceive what they are going through, have been through, are in for yet. It would cause OVERLOAD for you to fully fathom any life other than your OWN (or even your own). You don't even know your PARENTS or CHILDREN. You know them only AS parents and children. Siblings are no better. You may have shared a womb, a house, a garden, meals, Saturdays, Christmases, tortoises, schools, beds, clothes, books, crayons and toys, but all that just gets in the WAY later. As adults, you become for them a repository of SHAME, the only person who remembers their infant nakedness and hairdo blunders and tawdry criminal record. You LOVE them, sure – but you hardly know them.

It's our infernal IGNORANCE of others that allows

us all to DISAPPEAR, our tragedies only privately profound – to others they're just NEWS ITEMS or a JOKE. We don't see each other, we see only what failed to DISINTEGRATE at first sight.

The cool-looking cowboy guy in the street, passing Dot right by, really feels the cold. It is only with his cool grey-green cords and cool beat-up leather jacket and cool leather cowboy hat that he manages to keep WARM. He's going back to a flat he's been trying to sell for months. It's like living inside a FOLDER in a FILING CABINET, all sliding doors and mirrored walls and no natural LIGHT. The guy loves himself, innocently LOVES himself. He likes catching glimpses of himself performing every aspect of his existence, from making toast in the morning to touching his cock in bed at night. He opens ONE EYE when he wakes up, just to see himself SLEEPING. He has a beautiful garden he doesn't care about, a strange flat-faced cat he does care about, and a flat nobody wants to buy. After years of self-examination, he has drawn a BLANK. He is fodder for filing, a base life in a basement flat. What does he make of the world as he sips his Tio Pepe, outstretched in front of his modern mirrored mantelpiece?

Another one! Snappy dresser, over seventy, heavily moustachioed, unready for death, marching proudly into the stationer's. He is hunting down some ancient kind of typewriter ribbon with which he will complete his monumental history of Edinburgh. This project makes him feel terrifically SUPERIOR to every other man in the street. He alone knows how long the street has BEEN there, for whom it's NAMED (George) and why, and whether the arched vaults beneath it are about to crumble. But what will he EAT when he gets home? A ham sandwich? And will he think of his mother when the light falls a certain way? He recalls music at odd moments against his will. He knows not the joy of a MOZART song playing in your head; he is burdened with phrases from Elgar and Vaughan-Williams. Just before he dashes into the stationer's (who do not HAVE his typewriter ribbon), he looks with disdain at a kid on the street who he assumes should be in SCHOOL.

He's WRONG. This kid is on his way to a special School Support Scheme for teenagers who are otherwise about to be expelled from normal school. To allow for short attention-spans and dishevelled backgrounds, the classes start at midday. This boy's home life is INTOLER-ABLE. Nobody FEEDS him, nobody cares about him. Nobody notices if he's THERE or not, nobody notices if he's asleep or awake. Nobody knows how poignant he finds the back of his baby brother's head, and nobody ever will.

Perhaps they are all ASYLUM SEEKERS, the men in the street. One guy is. If he 'outstays his welcome', five policemen will break his door down, wrap him in a BODY BELT and wind thirteen feet of tape around his head. They do it ALL THE TIME. In bed at night he WRITHES WITH SORROW, remembering a dead aunt who loved him.

Yet, round us all there comes a pink snow of petals in spring. Sunlight dazzles at us through bushes. Water runs between our fingers. BIRDS see us. We are stared at by animals a lot. To them we probably seem a tightly knit bunch. WE see ourselves as almost entirely SEPARATE – except when you put your tongue in someone else's mouth and it tastes just like your own.

There are LOOKS exchanged in the street, looks between strangers. Sometimes a BABY looks me right in the eye! And I wonder if any of these people could stomach what I really AM. Terrible, to grow and walk and talk and eat and sleep and shit and fuck and give birth and DIE only to be a shame and disappointment to all who know me. PERVERSE of me to hang on for dear life!

SHIT IN THE CITY

With her attractive visage and personality, it was easy for Dot to make friends, especially in the New Town area, where her nasal English accent was no handicap. In fact she had hopes of being warmly welcomed by some Anglo-Scot in a Barbour jacket, ochre corduroy trousers, flat cap and a Range Rover at any moment.

She rented a little basement flat and could have been HAPPY, but her toilet was somehow connected to a waste pipe that ran through the whole building, a CLOACA MAXIMA that was now leaking RAW SEWAGE into Dot's HOME. Her redecorating plans were not just put on hold, they were somewhat REVERSED.

People shitting in a city. How many shits an hour? How many shits a MINUTE? Not just TWENTY or THIRTY, but HUNDREDS, hundreds of people shitting, hundreds of toilets flushing, the whole city pissing and shitting itself SILLY every minute, liquid everywhere, running through the body, through the buildings, streaming always downwards, and then back up in US.

It's probably easiest if you try to think of just ONE person shitting, then multiply this by ten, then twenty: TWO HUNDRED people on two hundred loos (unless they share), dealing, struggling in whatever way (you hope, ABLY), with their shit. For some this is the only shit of the day, for others just one amongst many. There is constipation in the city, there is diarrhoea, there is blood and piss and vomit. They can be MESSY, these outpourings. The world doesn't WANT them, but we give them anyway. If only it DID, we would seem so GENEROUS: sure, I'll shit for you today, NO PROBLEM, hold on to your hat!

So there they all are, struggling. Two hundred people, starting or finishing, straining, farting, yelping, reading, wiping. Let's assume they all stand up simultaneously and FLUSH. Two hundred flushes scattered about the city. But it's MORE than that. You must now multiply this intimate scene (assholes, soiled loo paper, locked doors) by ten, twenty, thirty! Two thousand, four thousand, SIX THOUSAND PEOPLE (with their newspapers) rising in secret from SIX THOUSAND SHIT-HOLES and flushing it all away.

Somehow the sewage system COPES. It doesn't have time to COUNT, it just TAKES it. Next minute, ANOTHER six thousand. Until there is a constant stream of gurgling faeces rushing through the metropolitan area! THIS is the true business conducted in a city each day.

A pretty woman struts by: Dot! She has pissed and shat her way through FORTY-FOUR YEARS. She has drunk coffee, tea, Coke, milk, juice, eaten noodles, taken

73

vitamins. She has no doubt been to school, participated in team sports, ridden a bicycle. She has sent the requisite thank-you notes of life. She has been loved, she has been disappointed, she is still confused. She has seen the sea. She is as ridiculous as you or I but acts SUPERIOR because she SHITS seldom!

Women are under such pressure to be PERFECT. An obvious way to achieve this is by not shitting! There's no HONOUR in shitting, you get no CREDIT for it! Anorexia has a lot to do with not wanting to shit. Those skeletal frames are an open declaration of the REFUSAL to shit and we're all supposed to ADMIRE and feel GRATEFUL: ah, thanks to Dot there'll be ONE LESS TURD in the world today. Hoorah!

It is so tiring looking at these gutless women poking at their salads while I attempt to claim my RIGHTFUL AMOUNT OF FOOD. Paris is full of them! Prancing around as if their lives are worth living. How COULD they be, amid all that pretty *pâtisserie*?

DOT AS A DECIMAL POINT
IN THE WRONG PLACE

Dot was getting her cunt noticed AT LAST, but the experience was not gratifying. She was lying on a hard hospital bed in the gynaecological department of the Edinburgh Royal Infirmary, receiving no compliments. Doctors and nurses were speaking to Dot from BETWEEN HER LEGS. They discussed the WEATHER and the NEXT APPOINTMENT as if they were all in some CAFÉ together – with Dot's belly as the table. At one point a doctor reached up towards Dot's left BOOB. He quickly withdrew his hand, but Dot knew: he'd expected to find his COFFEE CUP there.

They think they're easing your embarrassment by treating your privates as suddenly PUBLIC, a MEETING-PLACE in which to exchange light remarks and medical banter. But they're not easing you out of your embarrassment; they're easing you out of EXISTENCE. Once they've alienated you from your body it's easier to lever you off the PLANET.

The body is a JOKER, it toys with us, testing us, to

see how much we can TAKE. Dot couldn't take much at all!

What do you do when you find out you have a deadly disease? You SIT TIGHT, hoping it'll go away! It's not actually killing you yet, so you pretend it's not there and continue with your usual routine. It's some time later that you are forced to recognise you haven't carried off this miraculous feat: the disease is still there and it's now having a bearing on EVERYTHING. It took a while to absorb the news (SURPRISINGLY long) but now it's absorbed and it's having an IMPACT. You haven't sorted out a Will or taken lots of expensive trips or read all the books you always meant to read or done anything so CHEERING to others, were they to know you had only months to live. There is nothing CHEERING going on. You have not been BRAVE. You have simply become more self-pitying than ever before. You feel you have already lost everything, though this process is still to come. You are not worth KNOWING any more and have no one to CONFIDE in and live in a LIMBO LAND from not telling anyone. You have begun to FEEL ill, and you envy and resent everyone except those who are clearly suffering MORE than you: people who've been BOMBED or GARROTTED, or people with fatal diseases at a more advanced stage than yours. Your disease HUMILIATES you, so you try not to think about it. When you do, you feel like KILLING YOURSELF. When you have to see DOCTORS you feel like killing yourself.

Dot sought forgetfulness in the Water of Leith. Whenever there had been rain, the river rose and its waters turned milky brown. Seemingly ALIVE, it rushed along, water flowing always downwards – except when it hit a rock or a bank or the thin ridge of an island and flowed briefly UP. Squabbling ducks passed by at top speed.

In the winter she watched a blizzard from her semi-redecorated living room. The white dots seemed to hover close to the window-pane, staring back at Dot, before falling to their doom. No POINT in these dots.

Early on a peachy day, when the air was soft and damp and the sky shot out spurts of rain in a SEXUAL MANNER, Dot took a taxi to South Queensferry to see the BURRY MAN. This is a guy that emerges annually from a pub at 9:00 in the morning, covered from head to toe in green BURRS. Flowers are added on top of the burrs. It is unclear how he sees or breathes! He is held up on both sides by male escorts as he trudges through the town offering FERTILITY, collecting money for charity, being given whisky by people outside their houses (he has to drink it through a STRAW).

Dot trudged behind him for a while, picking up a few lucky burrs that had fallen off him on to the road. Then she got another taxi and went to the Forth Road Bridge, which is close to the Forth Railway Bridge but is NOT the Forth Railway Bridge.

The Forth Railway Bridge is a remarkable, wide-angled, almost ORGANIC structure in RED, with Victorian ENDEAVOUR and heroic ENGINEERING in its bones. It is the gargantuan equivalent of a tiny red SPIDER. It looks like it's collapsing all the time, it's so metallic and thunderous and kind of CURVY. Cormorants take

77

advantage of its nether regions, and the sound of trains going over it is GREAT.

The Forth ROAD Bridge is nothing like this. It was built in the 1960s for £20 million and it's a noteworthy sight if you're in FIFE and eager to get back to Edinburgh but up close it's a GREAT BIG BORE.

Dot walked out to the middle of the duller bridge, noting on her way the absence of any good graffiti. How can people have so little to say? she thought, as she climbed the railing. Below her, sunlight was hitting the boats on the Firth of Forth, making them glow bright white. The full moon was still visible to the west. Dot always chose good days to commit suicide!

People saw her clinging to the bridge and called the police. The area around Dot was cordoned off while the police tried to talk her down. Traffic was reduced to a SINGLE LINE IN BOTH DIRECTIONS, causing UNKNOWN HARDSHIP and TRAGEDY to commuters. As they drove slowly past Dot, people yelled out their windows, 'Jump, bitch!'

She jumped. And she smiled as she sailed downwards, always downwards, everything always downwards, knowing she was about to be OBLITERATED, her body released from its old order and scattered on the hard spiked swollen surface of the water. She had no regrets as she fell, but clasped her arms tightly over her breasts for fear of them being TORN OFF on impact. There are aesthetic considerations even in death. (Even in DOT.)

There was a tremendous PLOP as she hit the water: an imperfect performance. Gravity gets us all in the end.

JOHN FINALLY GOES SWORDFISHING!

While Dot died, John was sitting on a boat that was making its way back from Greenland. He was writing yet another letter to Dot's solicitor with poor sore hands.

Dear Sirs,

For the record, your client's name is not Dorothea de Radziwill Butser – it is Mrs Butser.

I was prepared for us to have a mutual consent divorce, though I wasn't happy about it.

But now you have led her to believe she can get some sort of fancy show-biz divorce and all my money.

Here's something I'll bet you didn't know about Mrs Butser. She turned my house into a ~~gazebo~~ bordello. While I was away fishing, for our mutual benefit, she was organising orgies with men I formerly trusted. One of them gave her a trestle table in recompense for her atrocities. He was forever

phoning up, presumably to arrange further assigna-
tions.

She says I'm unfaithful! The truth is, when the
going got tough, she scarpered – with £38,000!

So go ahead and sue me. I'm going to sue her!
And you!!!

After losing his job as a Careers Adviser (for advising too
many youngsters to go into PORN), John had become
a fisherman! It was a true penance. The boat was 73 feet
long and capable of speeds up to 12 knots. John was TER-
RIFIED by the size of the thing.

They worked for 20 hours a day, in swells of up to 30
feet. If a storm was approaching they had to dog down
every hatch, porthole and watertight door, check the bilge-
pump filters and fish out any debris from the bilge water.
Then they removed the scupper plates. WHATEVER. John
was sick as a dog most of the time. Covered with bruises,
he slept in his clothes. The SWORDFISH scared him,
lashing out at him with their swords like PIRATES as they
came on board.

But it was his hands in the end that really hurt. First
his right hand swelled up and started to THROB. He
held it above his head a lot, which seemed to help, and
used his left hand for everything. Then his left hand
began to hurt too. It was a relief when both became
NUMB.

John was baiting hooks and putting on light sticks when
he finally collapsed to his knees and WEPT, wept for his
life, for his hands, and his WIFE.

To his surprise and additional dismay, the other men came over and gave him a big GROUP HUG — they too had seen their fair share of schlock.

PART TWO

PART TWO

I will not flow for you into a bowl,
I will not empty out for you into a basin,
I will not depart upside-down for you.

The Egyptian Book of the Dead

THE CLOACA MAXIMA

I know what you think. You think you get to KEEP
YOUR BODY. You think you go shooting up a long
dark tunnel towards a bright light and when you reach
it you're surrounded by LOVE and dead relatives in white
gowns. You recover instantly from all your ailments, stroll
on over to the Pearly Gates, get judged and admitted.
Then you spend the rest of eternity listening to the
tinkling of tiny bells and the flapping of angels' wings
while you lounge absolved on well-kept lawns, ambrosia
and myrrh in abundant supply.

But what if souls float in solitary BUBBLES in the
afterlife, an unphysical ABSTRACT existence in some
kind of EGG? O egg, O egg. What a RELIEF, to live
without a body! No more nose-blowing, no more
DEFECATION, no illness, no hunger, no worries about
SELF-PRESERVATION and all the running, fighting,
hiding and SHOPPING that entails. No loud music in
restaurants (no RESTAURANTS), no Trash Night, no
TV, no taxes, no communication by NOTELET. No

punctuality problems – the final deadline has been met! No tears, no sleep, no night or day. No aspirin (but also no headaches!), no booze, no News, no pain, no fear. No smells or textures, no jokes, no PRIZES, no make-up, no reading, no itching, no adding or subtracting. No growth or shrinkage, no heat or cold, no land or sea, no plants and animals, no friends, no lovers, no bicycles, no sex, no DEATH. No paying of bills or brushing of teeth or changing of sheets or shovelling of snow or snivelling of kids. No GODS, no goblins, no milk or honey (none needed!), no Dante, no Beatrice, no Dido or Aeneas. No ELVIS. No Isis or Osiris either, no Anubis, no Shesmetet, no Nehebkau, no Renenutet, no Sobk, no Wepwawet, no Djafy, no Thoth, no Muhammad, no Messiah, no Yama, no Chitragupta, no Munkar and Nakir. No Granny and Grampops, no spirit guides, no harps or haloes, no seventy-two virgins, no scythe, no Styx, no NOTHING.

Just space, endless space, and you a sphere. Aware of other spheres perhaps but alone. Like water: bodiless, without will, flowing you know not where. Maybe we all get sucked down a PLUGHOLE, some kind of cosmic CLOACA (the universe must need good drainage), but it won't matter much.

Or what if it's just LIMBO LAND, no better or worse than THIS world, just a lot of unfriendly STRANGERS? What if the Underworld is a SLOW TORMENT of grouchy types who look disapprovingly at your choice of SANDWICH (as if it's not up to YOU what kind of sandwich you want to eat in the Underworld!)? What if the Underworld's full of people who've heard you FART, and REMEMBER it? Or TV licence snoops and traffic wardens, BUGGING you for eternity? Interview panels that never gave you a job, forbidding bus drivers, cranky stationery-shop employees who treated you like SHIT when you tried to order a new address stamp?

What if the Underworld's just LOW-KEY? Not dramatically bad but full of dreary fluorescent lights, the constant smell of CAT SHIT and the clackety-clack of hundreds of idiots using computer keyboards (they sound like mice MASTICATING!). No proper assessment of SIN, just a lot of anxious travel dreams on a repeating loop (lost passports, missed planes, abandoned offspring), and every day you have to go get some WOUND dressed by a sadistic nurse who YANKS the previous bandage off without pity and stuffs so much GAUZE into the wound (an orifice created for her pleasure) that it will NEVER EVER HEAL.

Instead of darkness or hell-fire, the merely unclear. Instead of authoritarian deities thundering around, PAPER-PUSHERS. Instead of pure fury and despair, petty gripes.

DOT IN THE UNDERWORLD

Midway in her life's journey, Dot had gone astray. She woke to find herself on a plane subject to turbulence. It flew past philandering husbands and the old ladies of Jaywick Sands, across cartoon landscapes and the stomach troubles of a lifetime, the vomiting, the diarrhoea, the rumbles and gurgles of a contorted intestinal tract, the agony this brings. Through the porthole she caught embarrassing glimpses of herself over the years, picking her nose or wiping her ass, drooling, sneezing, wanking.

They flew judderingly across a mountain of RAGE, stuff slithering down but forever re-forming itself, like a backwards volcano. A mountain of all the fury she'd ever felt, all the times she'd wanted to KILL, beat, pulverise, all the times she'd wanted to pound stationery-shop attendants' HEADS in with their own embossed address presses, and all the people who'd bullied, abused or DUMPED her without a qualm.

Beyond that was a steaming pool of shit, a sea of pee, a black lagoon of menstrual juices, pus, phlegm, snot, sweat, slime, nail clippings, dead skin cells and HAIR, an AMAZON BASIN of all the crap that had come out of Dot over her forty-four years.

Followed by the crap that went INTO her: unbelievable how much she'd downed, the BARRELS of stew, acres of potatoes, onions and carrots, caldrons of soup, the pounds of flesh and lard and all the unnecessary steaks and pies, the PIES! There was a mound of dried APRICOTS too, and an ominous field of hens and cows. Whole salmons she must have eaten lay gleaming, slapping their tails on the ground. And then the sandwiches, piled so high that some had fallen and caused a LOG JAM in the river of snot. THE SHAME OF IT!

Now the plane was flying over a desert land littered with the CLOTHES Dot had bought and never worn – Dot had been led like a LAMB by fashion. Shirts, tops, jackets, dresses, trousers, whole hillocks of TIGHTS, winter, autumn and spring coats, sweaters, shoes, boots, undies, accessories, all of which suddenly IGNITED in a mighty conflagration as the plane passed over them, designer labels or NOT, darkening the sky.

When the smoke cleared there was COLOUR, as if the desert had bloomed. But these colours belonged to an enormous JUNKYARD, composed of all the PLASTIC items Dot had used and discarded: toothbrushes, hairbrushes, combs, make-up and toiletry products of every sort, buttons, sun-glasses, pens, picnic cups, plates, cutlery, alarm clocks, records, Hi Fi equipment, cassette tapes (the Underworld has been TAKEN OVER by cassette tape – it hangs off everything like kudzu vines), dustbins, cling film, food packaging, soft-drink bottles, Barbie dolls and other toys, baby bottles, condoms, buckets, shower curtains, Band-Aids, carrier bags, suitcases, sandals, stupid ornaments, fake fruit and flowers and other home-decorating FIASCOS.

Next came a plateau of PAPER, a *massif central* of notelets, notebooks, postcards, photographs, diaries, documents, calendars, message pads, chequebooks, envelopes, application forms, loo paper, Kleenex, paper towels, food packaging, books, magazines, *papier mâché OBJETS*, pound notes and dollar bills, paper cups and paper plates, bus tickets, plane tickets, train tickets, parking tickets, receipts, recipes, paper bags, posters, cardboard boxes, playing cards, wrapping paper and suicide notes. Also all the newspapers she'd bought but never read (info of no ultimate value but current at time of purchase).

Next, a glittering array of the bottles she had recycled or NOT recycled. On all of this, across the vast plain (seen from the fast plane), fell all the rain and snow that had fallen on Dot during her lifetime, and all the waters that had tried to engulf her, from a bath in a basin as a baby, to a dip in the Mediterranean a mile from shore, an Arctic plunge in a pool at some sauna, and the many oceans she had crossed in planes. Also, the TEA she had drunk or not drunk, all those WASTED POTS OF TEA she'd made (without their COSIES on!), sloshing around down there under the zigzagging plane for HOURS, until it reached the brackish waters of the Firth of Forth which had done for Dot in the end.

INFINITE DOTS

Dot found herself in a dark wood. Two black horses cantered past. She tried to step back, but there's no stepping back from DEATH. A big guy with a scythe (yes, let's get it over with) cut her head off but it didn't hurt and she was able to find it and put it back on. Then he sliced her from crotch to collar-bone, and her GUTS fell out, which dismayed Dot because it was so MESSY, but she managed to scrape them up and shove them all back in.

Another guy lured her on to a boat. Not a FERRY or a BARGE, but a raked-stem, hard-chinned western-rig SWORDFISHING boat, 72 feet long with a hull of continuously welded steel plate and a 365-horsepower turbo-charged diesel engine capable of speeds of up to 12 knots. Its DOWNWARD push of gravity and its UP-WARD lift of buoyancy generated a TORQUE, which was called the 'righting moment'. Nonetheless, halfway across the Styx it sank.

Dot found she could breathe underwater! She wandered along the bottom examining things. Large fish passed, gobbling smaller fish who in turn were gobbling the smallest fish (there was a painstaking ORDER to the underwater world). Porpoises swam up to Dot but, finding her dead, shunned her. Starfish squirmed under her feet, terrified she'd use them DRIED for her interior-decor ideas. Fanned by manta rays, she walked past underwater WIGWAMS, sodden duvets and deck-chairs. From above drifted lit cigarettes which sparkled when they hit the sand. The starfish now turned into BIRTHDAY CAKES, one for each year of her life. Dot was longing for a cup of tea! Some fish eggs floated by, the size of tennis balls. Dot grabbed one and gingerly licked it, assuming this to be a dream.

She lived in a winkle shell for a while. She discovered she could enter into everything! She became a ROCK, and stretched out along her own fissures, feeling rocky. She was an old bored beech tree, her trunk painfully widening. She was a duck, in order to eat with a beak. She became a horse, to finally know what it's like to have hooves. She was a spider in a web, she was the web. She could be a flea, but preferred to be the air AROUND a bunch of fleas, tickled by their jumping. She wonderingly entered an ONION, as if it were a palace.

She was the left leg of a marionette. She inhabited an oboe as the helpless melody being puffed out. She was the type on this page for a while, but couldn't understand a WORD. She was all of ARISTOTLE and his philosophy. She was a cinema, the audience in her STOMACH, stereo sound coming from her lungs, her oesophagus projecting the movie on to the stomach lining. She jumped off mountainsides, was sluiced through dams, she sat (unseen) in burning houses and watched the occupants die. She passed right through a train carrying nuclear waste and felt only a brief ZING.

She could travel twice, THREE TIMES the speed of sound. For fun she leaned against a solar flare – it felt like a waterfall pounding on her back. Dot was the earth itself, with its hot and cold places, bare patches and hairy bits, gullies and protrusions: the whole Equator was an erogenous zone, wars were like an itch, and all she really wanted to do was SPIN.

You'd think that by now the world would be overrun with ghosts – so MANY dead! – ghosts everywhere, YOUR ghosts getting mixed up with MY ghosts, a hundred to every house, confusing everybody with their thumps and whispers and dropped crockery and eerie trails of smoke. Ghosts in grey, ghosts in green.

But in fact there's no profusion of souls in the afterlife. Somehow they all manage to knock along together and not get in each other's way. Maybe the Underworld's not just an IMMIGRATION POINT, a WEIGHING-STATION for moral corruption, where you hang around waiting to be forgiven for things. Maybe there's room in an infinite universe for a little MAGNANIMITY, and plenty of room for souls.

A SKELETON BAND

A skeleton band was playing. It's not just that they were under-supplied in the trombone department. The MUSICIANS were skeletons! They wore sombreros, some had shoes, but none of them had any FLESH. Every bone was out on show, some held on with coils of wire to keep them supple. Each musician had a little coccyx hanging between his legs. They were immodestly naked of LIFE. Their vertebrae trembled as they played.

Flesh is proud, bones are not – in mockery of us they wore clothes they didn't need. A woman standing near the band wore a low-cut dress that showed off her wind-dried white sternum. She held a cigarette in her pretty knuckle bones and raised a jaunty FEMUR under her skirt in revelry. Other bags of bones stood around swaying to the music, which was folksy rather than funereal. Dot was attracted by the catchy tunes.

As she approached, a young skeleton with a basket of fruit on his head cycled helter-skelter through the crowd. People playfully grabbed his fruit and pretended to eat it but where could food GO? They laughed without sound, kissed without tongues, fell clattering to the ground but jumped to their feet unharmed, give or take a fibula that was now the wrong way round, or a knee-cap swinging by a thread. The skeletons lacked an interior life that could be probed. You probe MUSCLE, FAT, cavernous GUTS and MINDS, not stacks of ribs with no belly button, like a cage with no canary. Love is bound up with the body. No love in the Underworld.

One bony lady, bedecked in a fancy bodice, garter belt and lace, kept bringing a frying pan down on her husband's bare skull, not once but a MILLION times – as if marital spats last an eternity and the afterlife were a SOCIABLE kind of place. As if death were not spent UNIMAGINABLY alone. The trumpet tooted, the drum echoed with a tat, violins were sawed, guitars rhythmically strummed. What the hell IS music anyway? Dot wondered. It seems to lead you towards the Underworld.

Dot was frightened by her present position in the scheme of things. She didn't WANT to be dead. She was tired of playing at being ROCKS. The only kind of existence that had any meaning for Dot was being ALIVE in the REAL WORLD. In her despair, she dropped to the ground and bemoaned her time on earth, and the day and the hour and the place and the seed and the womb that gave her life. *L'umana spezie e 'l luogo e 'l tempo e 'l seme.*

Through her tears she noticed a ghostly presence materialising before her. It turned out to be that of a flat-chested perky-nosed blonde who looked familiar but, being one amongst so many (so MANY) flat-chested perky-nosed blondes that Dot had known, Dot at first couldn't place her. 'Who are you?' she asked.

'My blood is English,' rasped the wraith (hoarse from shooting her mouth off all her life). 'I was bred in Notting Hill. I sang of interior decoration. I was on TV!'

'Belinda Lurcher!?' Dot exclaimed. 'But you're . . . a fountain of DIY advice! You can't be . . . *dead*.'

'Well, I'm not here on holiday,' growled Belinda.

'I'm so sorry. But it's lovely to meet you. I'm a great fan of your design ideas!'

Despite her deathly demeanour, Belinda could not help beaming a little. 'I have plans for this place too, you know. Yes, I intend to Lurchify Lucifer. I'll show you what I mean. Come, I'll be your guide.'

Few souls would feel confident about being taken through Hell by Belinda Lurcher – except Dot! She had always been happy to blindly lurch wherever Belinda Lurcher led, ledge by dark ledge. And Belinda had a CAR, which she drove from the BACK SEAT whilst painting her toe-nails. As she drove, she pointed out many design features of the Underworld. They've got some pretty funky stuff down there!

She dragged Dot into a cave full of BUN MOSS BALLS. Caves in the Underworld are called 'pouches', she explained. They had been mostly derelict when Belinda arrived, used only for escaping from sand storms. Now it was hard to find one that Belinda had not stripped and sprayed with silver glitter paint: the Underworld was in fact the IDEAL PLACE for Belinda Lurcher.

'I am one of these,' she said to Dot, holding up a bun moss ball.

DEATH STINKS

People are UNDERHAND in the Underworld. Underaged, underdeveloped underlings all, understated in their undershirts and UNDERSTANDING VERY LITTLE.

There are ADULTERERS in the Underworld, who want no one to be happy. Well-meaning adulterers who tortured women and their own FRIENDS when alive and still pine for adultery in death.

There are BEAUTICIANS in the Underworld, without their MAKE-UP kits (they really suffer).

There are IRONIES in the Underworld. For instance, you try your whole life to get AWAY from your family and then they all turn up in Hell. DOCTORS gather there too, feeling unwell.

But Dante was WRONG. It's not just a place for MISCREANTS. There are people in the Underworld who simply lacked PATIENCE, or listened to too much Radio Four. People who fell for the bunkum of RELIGION, people who killed spiders, spiders who killed

PEOPLE, goops who mocked Mozart. Mozart himself! The many vets who benefited from their clients' excessive DOG-LOVE. Cold, undermining sales assistants, sadistic nurses, and their VICTIMS. People who let their children play on railway tracks. People who loved the PHONE. People who WHISTLED (no need for this). People who worked for Disney in any capacity. Actors, farmers, nerds, fakes, sportsmen, cheapskates, world leaders, snobs, model-train addicts, clingy types, tragic tots, evil grannies, Scottish BAP bakers (no need for these). People who specialised in OPERATIC LAUGHTER. Guys who believed in GAIA. Guys who TALKED about their belief in GAIA. Bereavement counsellors, asbestos cowboys, punsters, Martial Arts boors, popes, millionaires, billionaires, the manufacturers of ARTIFICIAL FLAVOURS, people who cook nut loaves, orchestras, conductors, and orchestral music COMPOSERS (no need for this), postmen who hide the mail, patriots, spies, computer buffs, clowns, bullfighters, architects, columnists, chiropractors, Procurators Fiscal, Stipendiary Magistrates, royals, rude people, gym teachers. People who let their CHICKENS play on railway tracks. And men who hoick big gobs of phlegm up their throats as they're walking along the street and spit it so far that there's a noticeable PAUSE before you hear the plop.

There is a special rung of Hell for SCIENTISTS, who act in darkness. They play. Lord it over everybody as if they KNOW SOMETHING, even get PAID for it. Then out comes an ATOM BOMB (thanks) or a rabbit with pig's ears. They FUCK WITH THE PLANET. Napalm, uranium, plutonium, strontium – they can't get enough of the stuff. Dead scientists have to mingle with their VICTIMS in the afterlife, but generally they just sulk, unable to bear the fact they no longer have any power to FUCK WITH THE PLANET.

Retribution aside (though it IS tempting), the Underworld welcomes all. No real differentiations are made. Each dead soul is awarded the same futility. And all agree: DEATH STINKS. Dot, who had vestiges of religious training, had hoped there WAS no afterlife, for fear of being castigated there for having committed suicide, but it turned out that no death was deemed unworthy in THIS Underworld. It wasn't squeamish – it eagerly gobbled them all.

Belinda took her to a hellish subterranean CAR BOOT SALE in an underground car-park, an EVIL car boot sale full of STOLEN stuff snatched from the real world by poltergeists; enormous blue and yellow teddy bears and useless electric typewriters and pirated video tapes and not a bargain to be had. A silent resentful crowd moved through the winding aisles like shit shifting in a colon.

Dot found a TEA COSY! She didn't know what to do with it, since there WAS no tea in the afterlife and she had nowhere to put anything either. Belinda suggested Dot turn it into a RETRO tea cosy by stitching on a lot of black-and-white squares. Dot still didn't know what to do with it.

Belinda got all excited about a crate of CANDLES. How she had missed CANDLES. 'There is nothing like a candle in a corner to create atmosphere,' she informed Dot.

After placing lit candles behind tumbleweed in dozens of distant pouches (yes, we have Belinda Lurcher to thank for HELL-FIRE), they drove to an underground CAFÉ where you could get the only comestibles on offer in the Underworld: muddy brown Lethe water and flat square white mints (some with a cream filling). The place was packed with FASHION MODELS, who were stuffing their mouths and Gucci bags with mints. The models we see don't just LOOK dead, some really ARE dead. They leave the Underworld only to do their stint on the CAT-WALK, then return below, weighed down with designer clothing.

But they didn't die of ANOREXIA as everyone supposes. They died of BRONZING TREATMENTS, VITALITY DETOXES, MOTHERS-TO-BE SEREN-ITY FACIALS, COLONIC IRRIGATION, BIKINI WAXES and RADIANCE. That ain't no colonic irri-gation, honey, that ain't no BIKINI WAX. That's having the SHIT sucked out of you and the PUSSY ripped off you! And a mother-to-be serenity facial just means you get MUD slapped on your face because you got KNOCKED UP.

They died of EUPHEMISM. It would kill an OX.

DEATH IS DEBATABLE!

There's a Museum to Death in the Underworld. Glass cases, full of malignant tumours and poison rings and bullets that hit their targets, line the walls, interspersed with decorative displays of ancient weaponry. Belinda showed Dot how to press the buttons to hear people's last words or death rattles. Dot was particularly taken with a wall of suicide notes.

There were also goofy tableaux of famous people dying, acted out by the famous people themselves! Isadora Duncan could be seen getting her neck snapped every weekday, on the hour. Zorro was forever strangling himself, Faulkner fell off his horse again and again (he played it for laughs), and Arnold Bennett died repetitively of HICCUPS. It was VAUDEVILLE in there!

Belinda was bored by celebs other than herself, and hurt that no one had ever asked her to act out HER death (she'd been caught by the tide while hunting for shells to stick between panes of Perspex, which make attractive wall decorations, and she couldn't see why that wasn't AT LEAST as interesting as Arnold Bennett's hic-cups). She hurried Dot past Edward Gibbon with his exploding hydrocele so Dot never found out exactly what an exploding hydrocele IS. Tycho Brahe's bladder burst right in front of them but they just carried on, past Pliny breathing his last of Vesuvius' fumes, and Dostoevsky, who was trying to shift a bookcase to get at his pen, despite being specifically told not to by his doctors (played by shadowy holograms in the background). Belinda only slowed down to jeer at Coleridge.

'He just died ALL WRONG. He should have had the guts to jump romantically off a cliff or something in his heyday! Instead he clung on, taking drugs, borrowing money from friends, pissing off Wordsworth and suffering constantly from CONSTIPATION.'

Dot glanced at Coleridge who, though theatrically frozen in the act of picking up a bottle of laudanum, BLUSHED. Dot felt sorry for him.

'Perhaps he . . .' she began, but then hesitated, since she knew nothing whatsoever about Coleridge.

Coleridge himself came to the rescue. 'You were going to say, no doubt, that I accomplished more than many who were lucky enough to be endowed with looser bowels?'

'Uh, yes,' said Dot hesitantly. Coleridge winked at her and she was THRILLED, but Belinda impatiently pulled her into the next room where Attila the Hun was dealing with a bloody nose and Edward II had a red-hot poker up his ass. Dot detected a change of tone.

'Yes, we're nearing the prize-winners now,' said Belinda.

'Prize-winners?'

'Yeah, the prize for the most horrendous death,' said Belinda. 'It all gets decided in the Debating Chamber. I'll take you.'

Dot was tiring of Belinda and reluctantly followed her perky little ass out of the museum and up the street to another building of more functional design. They could already hear boos and cheers coming from the Debating Chamber. Inside, standing on a podium, a blood-drenched fellow was summing up the deaths under review.

'... cancer of the, uh, bladder, vulva, tongue and throat, always good contenders –'

'Hey, what about septic kidneys and an enlarged prostate? Come ON,' cried a disgruntled guy who was writhing around in the middle of the main aisle. 'What's wrong with THAT, I'd like to know.'

'That's nothing compared to being flayed alive,' mumbled a very red man behind Dot. He seemed to be oozing stuff on to the floor. Dot edged away.

'Things often descend into chaos,' Belinda explained, as if Dot didn't KNOW that by now.

On and on it went. There were many deaths to be considered. There were people in the room who'd been overwhelmed by wallpaper, vending machines and inflatable ELEPHANTS, people who'd been stabbed by raw spaghetti or Parmesan, and a dairymaid who'd been bowled over by a runaway cheese. Another girl had been kept waiting too long inside an airless stag-night CAKE. Various people had been killed by members of their own family for choosing the wrong TV show, not eating their porridge, or drumming non-stop. But you were GUARANTEED applause if you'd been stabbed in the eye by a violin bow, clawed to death by a peacock or pushed off a building by a SHEEP.

Belinda was bored by them all and gestured to Dot to follow her out. They went through a door at the back of the hall.

'Can anyone join in?' asked Dot shyly, wondering if HER death would get any sympathy.

'Sure. Except the cryonic guys, the ones waiting to be thawed when science advances enough. Because they're only half-dead and they act so superior.'

She pointed out a small square pool in a dark alcove. The green water glowed wonderfully and Dot ran up and dipped her fingers in. It felt warm, and tasted salty.

'Is this a spa or something? A healing bath?' she asked, hoping she would be allowed to swim.

'It's all the tears that have been shed over death,' said Belinda.

'How deep is it?'

'Bottomless!' said Belinda brightly.

This was too much for Dot. She'd HAD it. She was FED UP with the Underworld. Call this an Underworld? No heaven, no hell, no purgatory, no NUTTIN?

'GET ME OUTTA HERE!' Dot yelped, and fell, weeping, into the pool. The water felt warm but awfully STICKY and Dot had trouble getting out.

'Don't tell me you want to be reincarnated or something?' asked Belinda gloomily, as she gave Dot a hand.

This was the first Dot had HEARD about reincarnation and it sounded good to her! Whether she went back as Zorro or Marie Antoinette, she didn't mind, as long as she could be in the real world again.

Belinda felt cross. Why did her assistants want to be reincarnated all the time? She had really been hoping Dot would stay put and help with the makeover she was planning for Hell. There were so many BOULDERS that needed to be painted silver. And other exciting tasks. Belinda couldn't do it ALL...

Dot wanted to LIVE. But what does life matter, Belinda pointed out, if there's life after death? Why go back to all that PAIN and SORROW and the aggravation of being GOOD? Maybe none of it matters a jot. Or a dot.

THE THING ABOUT THE UNDERWORLD

The thing about the Underworld is that you have to fill
out so many FORMS. And they're full of impossible
questions, like your National Insurance number, your
NHS number, your father's date of birth, your mother's
mother's mother's country of origin. Not many in the
middle of their death throes think to bring all this information with them – but they sure WISH they had.

You fill out all the forms as best you can and hand
them in to belligerent BUREAUCRATS who hand
them right back, asking MORE questions. It is a silly and
childish GAME they play with you, it's INTOLER-
ABLE. As if you never existed if you can't remember your
Vehicle Registration Number! They don't actually CARE
who you are or what your Vehicle Registration Number
is, they are just trying to delay your rightful progress
towards REINCARNATION, for the HELL of it! The
thing is, if you can't prove you were BORN, you might
have to start over as a microscopic SPIDER or a PLANT.
That's how they run things in that old Underworld.

The bureaucrats were not only iffy about Dot's inability to remember NUMBERS. They require from murderers a list of their VICTIMS, just to keep records up to date. Dot was embarrassed to find that she couldn't remember a single old-lady name!

Belinda took pity on her. 'If you're really determined to be reincarnated, you have to go back as a ghost. It's not so bad. But the sooner you go the better, before your family shreds all your credit cards and throws out your scrap book. People are always rushing to tidy up after a death.'

N.B. This is why ghosts are seen wafting around their old homes: they're looking for their FUCKING BIRTH CERTIFICATE, the original not a photo-copy. It's surprising that seances aren't jammed with spirits asking, 'What the hell did you do with my HANDBAG/BRIEFCASE/WALLET/DRIVER'S LICENCE/EXAM RESULTS?'

After climbing into her GHOST outfit (kind of like a DIVING suit and rather clammy), Dot set off in another plane. A LOT of turbulence on this flight: the winds are all in the wrong direction when you're coming BACK from the Underworld (it's supposed to be a one-way trip).

It can be really problematic EMOTIONALLY for sui-cides to return to the real world, the world they just REJECTED or that rejected THEM. But nobody cares about that in the UNDERWORLD, nobody gives a DAMN about you in the Underworld. Dot clutched her forms and hoped for the best.

On landing she was able to verify by the dullness of her surroundings that she was indeed in Jaywick. Grey day, flat horizon, mud colours. She was struck by how EARTHBOUND everything seemed, how STUCK. We're held so tightly to the earth. She'd forgotten what it was like to be imprisoned inside a body that needed to breathe air and pump blood around and digest and excrete and walk and rest. She had never noticed how glued DOWN we are by the demands of gravity: trees, houses, animals, water, even refrigerators, all PINNED to their allotted spots. We only scuttle HORIZONTALLY, if at all. Even birds don't escape very far.

John was in bed with Julie when Dot wafted in. Julie was blindfolded and tied to the bedposts and John was carefully positioning a pillow under her ass. But Dot was quite calm; she just wanted her PIN number and some names of old ladies. She slunk ethereally around the house looking for John's address book, and gave a miniature orange plant Julie had bought such a chill (accidentally), all the miniature oranges dropped off. Dot searched for the address book under furniture, in amongst papers, on shelves, in drawers and cupboards. If John and Julie heard weird noises, what did that matter to DOT? But when she went bumping past the humping pair to look under the bed she must have made too much of a commotion, since Julie exclaimed through her GAG, 'Wha' the fu's tha'?' Somehow, John SENSED that it was Dot and cried out bewilderedly, 'Dot?!' Julie started squirming around in muted horror. Dot gave her suspender belt an eerie TWEAK but there was no time for further frivolities.

Dot eventually found the address book in the kitchen drawer (which was shockingly messy). The old ladies were easily identified because John had drawn a red line through their names, indicating death. He'd drawn the same sort of line through DOT's name and her address in Edinburgh. But, just by chance, long ago, he'd written down her PIN number, Vehicle Registration Number, credit card number and expiry date, the code for telephone banking and OTHER JUNK. What a haul! John had redeemed himself! Dot felt a real glimmer of warmth towards him, and to show her appreciation, as well as to scare them again, she put the address book in the TOASTER and gave it a light browning.

On her return, after being kept on hold and having BAD MUSIC played to her for an eternity, Dot was finally given permission to join the crowd that was awaiting reincarnation. She found herself seated next to a Russian girl who'd died of exposure from sitting all night on a couch after her boyfriend dumped her. She was still wearing the same clothes she'd died in: COTTON SHIRT, BARE MIDRIFF, and JEANS decorated with paper straws all round the waistband. Dot was tempted to say that this was no way to dress in Russia! But she stopped herself. Perhaps the girl would get a BETTER life this time around. People are so quick to dismiss death as a BAD thing.

O EGG, O EGG

Wombs are of great interest in the Underworld – they're the only way out of the TOMB! WE no longer see sex as anything to do with engendering life, but that's how it's viewed in the Underworld. Sex only EXISTS because of death. They wait, they watch, a queue of souls bickering over who'll get to inhabit the next fertilised egg. No sexual act is frowned upon THERE. Each copulation is greeted with cries of RELIEF and HOPE.

What do WE care about the preservation of the species, eh? Sex has lost all heroism for us. But in the Underworld it's considered COMMENDABLE, a charming ritual that smooths over all the preceding bureaucratic wrangles. Reincarnation is so COMPLICATED, conception comparatively simple: not many decisions to be MADE except how rushed, how rough, how sweet.

Once assigned an egg, you have to drink muddy brown water from the River of Lethe to make you forget the Underworld and your previous life (any mention of the Underworld or afterlife or GHOSTS will be treated as a JOKE in the real world, so it's important that you too can mock them convincingly).

The boat was covered with shells now, courtesy of Belinda Lurcher. They even had a light dusting of silver sparkle spray-paint on top. Dot handed her obol over to Charon and clambered on board, barely able to contain her joy. Everyone was clutching little bottles of Lethe water. Dot was glad to see the Russian girl was drinking hers: soon she would forget all her troubles.

The boat sank under the weight of all those shells, but no matter. They walked the rest of the way. When they dragged themselves up on to the opposite bank, the earth already felt more SOLID.

Everyone was very excited, but they had to wait around outside the Fur Factory first, while animals chose their markings for the next life (yes, dogs with a nice black spot over one eye CHOSE that). The wait gave Dot a chance to consider her position. She had FUMED about the delays and corruption in the Underworld, but now that the time had come to LEAVE she felt a little nervous. Could a new life really be worth all the PAPERWORK? And no one had asked her yet WHO she wanted to be. Why wasn't anyone taking her order? She didn't mind, as long as she was someone FAMOUS. (She'd only ever heard of famous people being reincarnated so this didn't seem too much to ask.)

Finally everyone was directed over to a row of giant funnels that hung from the sky. They looked INDUSTRIAL and kind of BEAT UP, and seemed to be made of dented tin or aluminium. Everybody stared at them dubiously, but in the end they did as they were told and huddled underneath while the machinery warmed up. Then, one by one, souls slowly drifted up into the funnels! It was somewhat UNDIGNIFIED, Dot felt. But you put up with a LOT in the Underworld.

DOT REBORN!

Once she was inside the funnel, the suction seemed to increase, to an almost unbearable level. She was moving swiftly up a long grey tunnel. Far ahead she could see a small square door. It was yellowish, and had curved edges. Dot wondered briefly if Belinda would approve of this yellow, before she forgot Belinda completely. She wasn't aware of having gone *through* the door – perhaps she fainted? – but the next thing Dot knew she was warm and wet and nestling amid soft dark blobs. SUCCESS: Dot was a BLASTOCYST.

She had never known such peace, such freedom from responsibility! No dishes to be done, no sins to repent, no thank-you cards to write. Just herself alone, a SPHERE, in a warm bath of blood. She lazed around, no, REALLY lazed around, for DAYS. No sights, no smells, no tastes. She gradually forgot such things existed. It was PARADISE.

Then she was EXPELLED. Dot was furious. There must be some mistake! She couldn't have been there more than eleven, twelve, maybe thirteen days – Dot wanted the full nine months!

But there was no mistake. Dot had been awarded the next available ovum (this was what she'd signed up for on some form or other), which happened to be that of a MARSUPIAL. Dot was a possum!

Without any time to prepare herself for the birth trauma, Dot was blasted from her mother's aching cloaca. Dot was now supposed to claw or paddle her way to the POUCH (something Dot had never done before and was no GOOD at). In some disarray, Dot contrived to FALL OFF. With most marsupial families (not dysfunctional, just rather BUSY), this might have been a fatal mistake, but Dot's mother happened to NOTICE Dot wiggling around on the ground and wanted to help her. So she LICKED Dot, and continued to lick her until Dot ESCAPED this licking by jerking, curling and straightening her bug-like body and swinging her strong little arms. In this way, Dot eventually managed to put a distance of 2 CENTIMETRES between herself and her mother.

Her mother moved closer to Dot and SAT DOWN. Dot thought she would be crushed, CRUSHED, but wasn't! Instead she now felt warmth and fur and knew enough to grab at it, and thereby got hold of her mother's tail. So Dot finally began her epic journey to the pouch! If you discount all the initial flopping around, she reached it in record time: $16\frac{1}{2}$ seconds! Her mother had SAVED HER LIFE.

All Dot had to do now was find a TITTIE. But a

whole crowd of embryonic siblings had beaten her to it. Each had a teat firmly clamped in its mouth. By clawing, squirming, scratching, straining, sort of SWIMMING, yanking her way along, Dot eventually found one too. She was safe! She had everything she needed: milk, warmth, comfort, a mother who had SAVED HER LIFE, and surprisingly little oxygen (but she didn't need much).

There is something cosy about a pouch, that outside womb, something a little TEA COSYish. You could have put Dot and her siblings in a TEASPOON! People are always DOING this to possums, to prove they are the size of a PEA or a BEE. Just a blob of life, a spot of bother. A dot in the universe.

Dot's mother was a Virginia Opossum but she lived in Ohio. Like other Virginia Opossums she had a whitish snout and a grey body. The fur stopped halfway down her tail so that she could grip things with it and hang upside-down. Her ears were misshapen from frostbite, but otherwise she was healthy. She had FIFTY TEETH and her favourite meal was: wasps, centipedes, a box turtle and some wild cherries. Dot's father's favourite meal was a garter snake followed by grasshoppers. They caught sight of each other one day behind a mulberry bush and mated quickly, lying on their sides. Then he disappeared. He didn't phone, he didn't write.

She found a nice cave in which to give birth. Possums trust anything pouchlike. They look for caves or holes or tunnels whenever they're in trouble (they only 'play possum' as a last resort).

Dot was her mother's TWENTY-THIRD CHILD

in an unceasing series of nurturings, a CARICATURE of motherhood (the monstrosity of it all). Dot's mother had carried her last litter in the pouch until she could no longer MOVE and the pouch was dragging on the ground and the babies were all STICKING OUT, baby possum asses everywhere. Later she got them to ride on her BACK, which was slightly easier.

DOT'S MOTHER WEIGHED DOWN BY POSSUMS IN THE POUCH

DOT'S HALF-BROTHERS AND SISTERS RIDING ON DOT'S MOTHER
(BEFORE DOT WAS BORN)

DOT'S INFANCY

Once Dot forgot all about being reincarnated and was getting used to being a possum, she sucked her milk with gusto and was content. She was EMBRYONIC after all and embryos are PRETTY EASY TO PLEASE. Dot knew nothing but MILK and FUR and POUCH. She didn't even know if she was male or female (her BODY had barely decided), and she didn't CARE.

Her mother made loud clicking noises as she went about her business in the woods and brambles. Sometimes she scrambled jarringly up a tree. But Dot didn't mind. She had a tight hold on her teat and some fur and never let go. She was only vaguely aware of her siblings who, like Dot, were now starting to grow their blond baby fur. They all hung on.

Everything was going fine until Dot's mother was caught in a TRAP. She wasn't skinned or made into Possum Pie, but instead shipped – alive – to Yale University for the purposes of scientific RESEARCH. Dot's mother had the misfortune of belonging to a species of interest to scientists, on account of her urogenital system: in a caricature of womanhood, the monstrosity of it all, Dot's mother had TWO VAGINAE and TWO UTERI.

Each uterus was a fusiform body, elongated caudally into a narrow uterine neck. The necks of both uteri ran parallel for 3 millimetres, ensheathed in a common mass of connective tissue. Each uterine neck opened into the vaginal cul-de-sac of its own side at the *os uteri*, situated ventrolaterally on the uterine papilla. The median septum between right and left vaginal cul-de-sacs arose in the midline at the junction of the uterine papillae. The anterior vaginal canal of each side merged with the lateral vaginal canal which was long and convoluted. Posterior to the bladder the two lateral vaginae and the urethra joined to form the urogenital sinus which was long relative to the anterior components of the system.

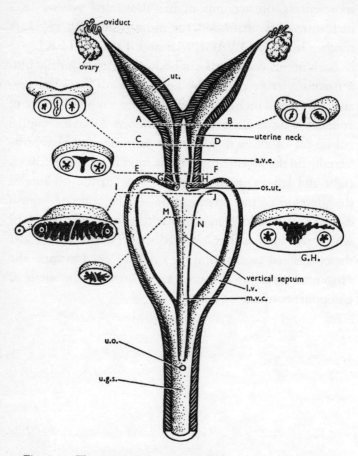

Fig. 1. — The urogenital system of Dot's mother. The various transverse sections *AB*, *CD*, etc. are not drawn to scale. *a.v.c.*, anterior vaginal canal; *a.v.e.*, anterior vaginal expansion; *bl.*, bladder; *cl.*, clitoris; *l.v.*, lateral vagina; *m.v.c.*, median vaginal cul-de-sac; *os. ut.*, os uteri; *p.v.s.*, posterior vaginal sinus; *r.s.*, receptaculum seminis; *u.b.*, position of opening of ureter into bladder; *u.g.s.*, urogenital sinus; *u.o.*, position of opening of urethra into urogenital sinus; *ur.*, urethra; *ut.*, uterus.

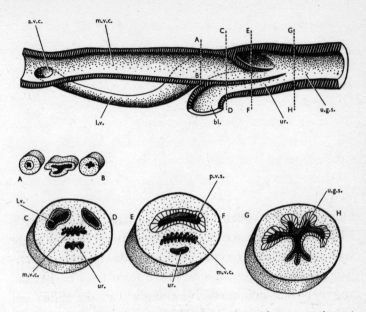

Fig. 2. — Longitudinal section of vaginal complex with cross sections at various levels. Symbols as in Figure 1.

FUCK SCIENCE

Dot would have been FINE, would have had a GREAT LIFE as a possum, wandering around eating bugs all night with her crocodile mouth, sleeping all day in some pouch-like burrow, hanging upside-down from trees by her tail and opposing her opposable thumbs. But she didn't get to because SOME SCIENTIST wanted to study Virginia Opossum pouch young. Any baby possum would do. Some used in the study hadn't even attached themselves to a teat yet – they were still coming down one vagina or the other when the mother was killed. Others were just born and were found crawling in the dead mother's fur, LOOKING for the pouch.

All in all, the scientist collected (KILLED):

23 maturing preovulatory oocytes
38 uncleaved fertilised or unfertilised eggs
17 cleaving eggs
27 unilaminar blastocysts
32 bilaminar blastocysts

36 trilaminar blastocysts
22 foetal embryos
51 advanced foetal intrauterine stages
100 newborn young
100 pouch young

All that marsupial MIGHT wasted, the wonder and efficiency of it all. Dot's infantile happiness THROWN AWAY, so that some guy could better understand marsupials. But do marsupials understand US?

Dot was still attached to the teat she liked so much. But the scientist wanted to understand how she was attached to it EXACTLY. So he did a cross section of the nipple, slicing right through Dot's head as she sucked.

This was of limited benefit to SCIENCE, but it sure meant a lot to DOT. For she was back in the Underworld, this time as an embryonic possum that looked like a BUG, a tiny blonde fuzzy DOT that could only grab at things and squirm around and suck. She had to negotiate the Underworld like this, sightless and AGAIN with no National Insurance number. Belinda Lurcher wouldn't even come near her, Dot was so lowly: she was a Lesser Mammal after all.

Dot DIED for this:

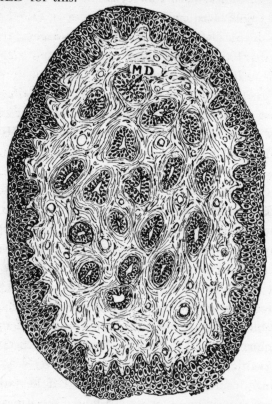

Figure 48. — Transverse section of the nipple of an opossum. The young one had been recently born and was hanging to the nipple. The specimen was prepared by cutting thin slices through the head of the young animal, the nipple being sliced as it was held in place in the young animal's mouth. The slice is shown as seen under a microscope. Eighteen little ducts (M.D.) convey the milk along the nipple to the offspring.

You know, chicks have a DARK SIDE. They look help-less and fluffy but actually they're kind of SCRAWNY under all that fluff and they can PECK. Sheep recognise each other from PHOTOS. They EXIST. To each other animals are wholly real. The earth and sky are real to them, their bodies, pain and pleasure, their mothers, their children. It's all perfectly real until WE take it away.

WHY is there no place for animals in our Underworld? The Ancient Egyptians had all kinds in theirs: the ostrich, duck, goose, pigeon, pelican, vulture, heron, falcon, eagle, guinea fowl, ibis, flamingo, swallow, bee, fish, worm, eel, crocodile, scorpion, dung beetle, python, cobra, panther, lion, leopard, jackal, cat, dog, mouse, cow, ox, pig, antelope, hippopotamus, donkey and baboon all get a mention in *The Book of the Dead*. Mexicans too expect to find animals in the afterlife: the dog you kicked here will be there to bite you. What do WE get? Barren rock, fire, devils, tor-ment and remorse. Dante mentions animals (a leopard, a lion, a she-wolf) but they're only there to serve US, or to SYMBOLIZE something.

What if we had to ANSWER to animals some day for what we've done to them? What if they demanded retribution? Put us all in PENS, with our shit falling through metal grates on to sawdust below, no room to TURN AROUND? What if they took all our EGGS away? What if they lined us up and slaughtered us one by one in front of our friends and family, so that they could EAT us? What if they yelled at us for peeing indoors, stuck fire-crackers up our asses, or flung us down apartment-block stairwells for fun? What if they castrated men and artificially inseminated women? What if they fed us human flesh to FATTEN us quicker? What if they MILKED us (DAILY)? What if they stuck BITS in our mouths, whipped us and made us CARRY them places, or forced us to jump over HURDLES that broke our legs? What if they clothed themselves in our hair and skin, made pillows from our down, BOILED OUR BONES to make Jello desserts for themselves? What if they ROASTED us with apples in our mouths and the LEG MUSCLES OF OTHER PEOPLE draped across our backs? And considered our foetuses and testicles a special delicacy? What if they watched NATURE SHOWS on TV about us mating or fighting and COOED over cute footage of our babies, while cramming their mouths full of us, sliced? What if they REALLY GOT THEIR OWN·BACK – and justified it on the grounds of THEIR science and religion, which confirmed we were there to be used?

What if WE were sent down mines to test the air? What if whales blew US up if we happened to beach ourselves on some shore? What if dogs sat in the sledge while WE pulled, or made US smell suitcases for bombs or sent US barefoot into burning buildings to help DOGS get out alive? What if donkeys made us pull WHOLE HOUSES for them, and cats put our babies in bags and drowned them? What if we had to accompany animals to THEIR wars?

What if they put us in zoos and STARED at us, or tried out every goddam chemical in our eyes? What if they stuck jellyfish genes in us to make us GLOW, or cloned us and harvested our organs for the benefit of PIGS? What if they permanently catheterised WOMEN to make HRT for mares?

What if lobsters rose up and BOILED US ALIVE, and oysters ate us raw and wriggling, with a dot or two of Tabasco? What if chickens put OUR day-old infants on conveyor belts and sent them sliding down chutes and twirling through funnels to a battery-farm future? What if bulls won all the BULLFIGHTS and rabbits pulled us out of hats?

What if they let their children secretly TORMENT us? What if they FRIGHTENED us continually, stole our land and FUCKED us whenever they liked?

The Arts barely acknowledge the EXISTENCE of animals (unless you count Stubbs, Saint-Saëns, sadistic cartoons, Aesop's fables and that lousy *White Fang*). It's all got to be about US: endless tales (SO MANY TALES) of us managing to meet up and mate, and paintings of us getting undressed, or killed, or RICH. What is the point of encouraging our CHILDREN to like animals, giving them pets and toy bunnies, and reading them animal stories, when, as adults, they will only KILL, EAT, and ABUSE animals and buy animals for their own children to abuse, eat, kill?

Scientists are so SMUG, so sure they're RIGHT, so sure that they KNOW something. Medicine's their big success story. So where's the cure for cancer? People still die of FLU! Scientists only want to SUBDUE us and create Weapons of Mass Destruction. THEY should be destroyed, THEY should be dissected, not given PRIZES and interviewed on the radio by awestruck laymen.

They *know* they're doomed: scientists out in public are always looking over their shoulders, like presidents ripe for assassination. They KNOW their systems suck and they're failing us.

What's Science ever done for the Rare Spotted Cuscus except CUT IT UP and give it a Latin name (*Phalanger maculatus* – yeah, great)? What's Science actually done to stop everything going WRONG? Where's Science when there's a strange man FARTING IN YOUR BED? Where's Science when you're nearing SIXTY, still craving your dead father's approval (though you'd make do with your FATHER-IN-LAW's)? Where's Science when you're walking down a hot city street after drinking too much MADEIRA?

WHERE THE FUCK IS SCIENCE?

The whole world respects ONLY Science now! Every spare penny goes on keeping it afloat. Science will OUT-LIVE us, their computers babbling to each other and checking themselves for viruses long after WE'VE ALL DIED of the drugs scientists invented and the radiation they released. What good will it do us then that they classified every species or built AEROPLANES? That won't bring your dearest AUNT back. It won't illogically remind you of APRICOT NECTAR.

Seek wasteland, seek wilderness. Cling to anything they haven't EXAMINED yet.

DOT WINS A PRIZE!

Belinda's makeover was complete: she had filled the Underworld with low-voltage halogen lighting, chrome cladding, sequinned tumbleweed, *faux* tortoiseshell, sanded floorboards and glass-topped tables. In her new embryonic form, Dot kept slipping on the tables and getting splinters from the floorboards! She was lost for a time amongst a decorative corner display of BUN MOSS BALLS.

How to apply for reincarnation when one is so LOWLY? But Dot was in luck. News of her death filtered down into the Underworld. Dot was eventually located and rushed to the Debating Chamber, just in time to be awarded the prize for the most horrific death that week! She was carried aloft down the centre aisle but nobody could SEE her so they put her down on the podium and asked her what she'd like as her reward.

In a tiny voice, Dot replied, 'I want to be REBORN … as a … PERSON.'

Everyone cheered. The paperwork was completed for

her, and the bureaucrats were somehow placated. Dot signed the forms with a miniscule right paw, and then she was escorted to the boat by a skeleton band playing 'I'll take you home again, Kathleen'. Her obol was paid by the Prize committee, and Dot was soon on the other side of the Styx.

At least she had specified this time that she wished to be HUMAN. But once again she was baffled that no one asked her WHICH human she wanted to be. There were other worries too. A lot of complaints were coming in from SHEEP, who kept being made sheep AGAIN. There was a Foot and Mouth Crisis going on and they didn't WANT to be sheep! You were barely BORN before you were thrown on the pyre. These sheep were so desperate they said they'd even be willing to be PLANTS (NOBODY wants to be a PLANT).

Other animals were murmuring darkly about anatomical remnants of PREVIOUS LIVES: a horse, reborn as a mouse, had found he could still whinny and his neck was too LONG; an ostrich was surprised to see fur growing under her wings; and a crocodile came back as an alligator and couldn't tell the DIFFERENCE.

All reincarnations ceased while important work was carried out on the funnels. It was a tense time. But finally, operational efficiency was restored and Dot and several sheep were offered a trough of Lethe water to drink, a sign that soon they would be setting off on a new life (the sheep still hoping not to be sheep). The mood was optimistic.

Reincarnation IS for optimists!

Spiral of personal Horrors

cartoon landscape

Mountain of Rage

Excremental Pool of Bodily Waste

The Food she Ate

The Clothes she Bought

(flames starting)

The Plastic she Used

133

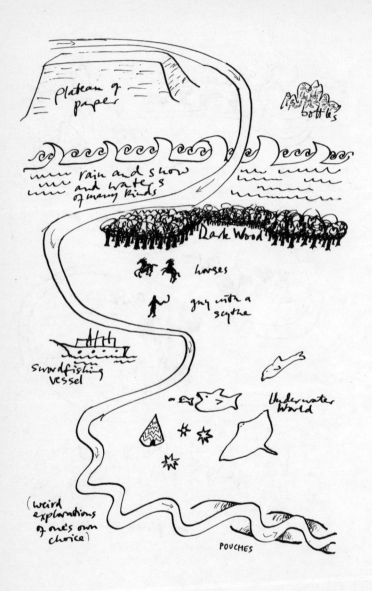

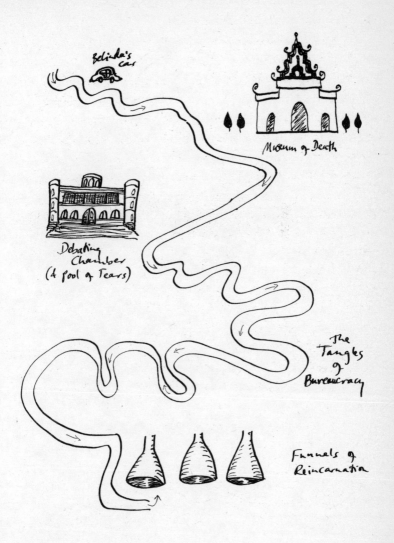

Belinda's car

Museum of Death

Debating Chamber
(A Pool of Tears)

The
Tangles
of
Bureaucracy

Funnels of
Reincarnation

PART THREE

Life is understood backwards,
but must be lived forwards.

Kierkegaard

DOT REBORN (AGAIN!)

America does suburbia so well! No one else knows how to drive that much truth and beauty out of life. They think, with their cars and their condos, their low-cholesterol dips and chips, their dumb-ass religions and daughters-in-law, their knowledge of several kinds of spaghetti sauce, their wasteful use of gas, electricity and hot water, their dependence on STYROFOAM, their Bargain Basements, sprinklers, jungle gyms, their screens-vs.-storm-windows understanding of the seasons, their card games, calorie-counting and cancers, their all-you-can-eat Sunday brunches, they think THIS is enough to overcome the meaninglessness of the universe! (Or have they simply accepted it?)

There are three types of house: ranch, colonial or modern (fake thatched roofs made of ASPHALT are optional). Whichever one you've got, a basketball hoop hangs over the garage. You rake leaves, shovel snow, and mow the lawn, depending on the time of year. And somewhere near by there's a Mall, where you can buy everything you want and if you can't FUCK YOU: a Chaplain at one end, False Memory Stirrer at the other, Blood Pressure Checkpoint in between. WHOLE LIVES are conducted here – you never need leave as long as you keep buying SHOES. You can eat breakfast, lunch and dinner in the Food Court: there's an ice-cream place with every kind of ice-cream and a bagel place with every kind of bagel. People EXERCISE by walking around the Mall in official exercise GROUPS.

Every Mall has a supermarket dedicated to oral delight and unsustainable resource. There you will find Big Grab Bags and Big Gulp Drinks, or a Deluxe Fruit Basket done up with a pretty pink bow, 'generously packed with fresh mountain Pears and Apples, and loose-skinned Mandarins with a rich smooth citrus flavor' (the only loose-skinned thing that ever sounded good, besides an elephant). The AIMS of suburbia are in evidence everywhere, on the menus, the birthday cards, coupons, ads for the bank, frozen-pie cartons: the perfect HOUSE, the perfect FAMILY, the perfect MILKSHAKE, the perfect LIFE. All varying in significance but equal in perfection.

Milkshake ÷ perfection = perfection.

But there is no perfection here! It's like the fall of the Roman empire – everyone is so FAT. America's the only place in the world where fat people feel comfortable. They have RIGHTS. Things are adjusted to accommodate them. In America fat people even get MARRIED. They do all the stuff thin people do, except maybe slower. They flirt, run companies, play baseball, relax HALF-NAKED on BEACHES. They have no idea what's going on in the rest of the world (they read only local papers) and they don't WANT to. They exist only to stuff WHOPPER SUBS into themselves in order to achieve ever-greater INSENSIBILITY.

The suburban idea of conversation: vivid description of a daughter-in-law's allergic reaction to CALAMARI (wooziness followed by nausea, vomiting and diarrhoea: it is stressed that both ends of the alimentary canal were called into play during the crisis). Someone chips in with HER daughter-in-law's response to SHRIMP (face swells up and liquid issues from every pore). They're big SURVIVORS, Americans. They'll gross you out into eternity.

In a spiral of EATING, TALKING about food, BEING fat, and giving FOOD away to the POOR, they somehow convince themselves they have free will. What they have is a PLAGUE.

There ARE real tragedies in America, but nobody wants to look at them. There are real successes and real failures, but nobody knows which is which.

And yet, an unobtrusively well-organised life could be had in suburbia in the '50s and '60s, with Leftover Night every Thursday and a view of sunlit grass or snow out the kitchen window, the house angled to see the woods behind it.

In a suburb of Cincinnati, Ohio, amid other suburbs of Cincinnati, Ohio, sat a house that was DIFFERENT from all the other houses in all the other suburbs of Cincinnati, Ohio. It contained everything GOOD that America can be! Dot knew this house so well that in later life she could comfort herself by walking around it in her mind, stand looking at the little stained-glass birds, boats and balloons that hung on the back door and glowed as the sun set behind them. See the neat china basin and pitcher on the antique wash-stand that housed the liquor bottles, the souvenir glasses on the windowsill over the kitchen sink, the weird gangly plant by the stairs to the attic, the rocking chair with its plaid cushion, the giant black ants that came out from under the kitchen cupboards, the trash closet with treasured newspaper clippings and recipes taped to the inside of the door. She could walk down the hall on the plaited rag rug her mother had made in the first year of her marriage, past the Den on the right where her father liked to paint, past the little pale-yellow bathroom on the left, with its shell-shaped soaps and view of trees outside and low loo and soft loo paper and pale-yellow hand towels (blue for guests), past the box-framed picture at the end of the hall containing REAL LENTILS and PASTA and tiny dried purple flowers. To her parents' room, so QUIET, the high bed with its white quilt, big paintings on the wall, and the two little windows from which Dot's mother once, when ill, saw car thieves trying to drive across the front yard and made a CITIZEN'S ARREST through the WINDOW, while Dot's father called the police. There was a lot of SUFFERING in this room, but it retained its perfection in Dot's mind: the bed they shared, the rag rugs,

Christmas presents bought well in advance and hidden in the closets, ice-cream every night with the Eleven O'Clock News on TV, the frilly curtains her mother had made and the blinds with their rings on strings.

Her father's paintings everywhere, the revolving steam-train lamp, the sofa in the living room that turned into a bed. The SAGA of the ant infestation and her mother's war on them. The smell of coffee and cigars, the plentiful but dutifully measured whisky and sodas when people came, all meant so kindly! – in the wooden house like a New England BARN up on its hill at the end of the quiet street.

Dot's parents – Maisy: plump white shoulders Dot loved, blonde hair, cigarettes, high heels and red lips; and Sam: anxious, funny, wild-haired, often leaping up to change the record or check something in the dictionary, still clutching his cigar. They had LOVE OF LIFE. It had blossomed somehow in OHIO, summers spent wiping sweat off your nose bottling tomatoes, winters knee-deep in snow. They had wanted only to be together, and had children as a happy afterthought to their love. Doomed to DIE IN DISARRAY, she slightly before him. But what does the END matter if your heart went into the beginning and the middle?

They were an amalgamation of natural substance, carbon atoms, European descent, American innocence. Maisy saw Sam's legs lit by the headlights of his car when it broke down on their first date, and knew she loved him. He loved her hair, which she kept in a loose bun except in bed, when its gold encircled her. This, and her lips, her thighs, her calves, her breasts, would serve him all his life. They honeymooned in Mexico.

Sam was a psychoanalyst with no respect for his patients. They all seemed too rich and spoiled and STUPID to have real problems. He would come home and RAIL against America, its government, culture, idiocy and self-love. He was suspicious of American thought, American FOOD, American fads, the movies, cartoons, schools, the Army, the meat industry, ALL institutions, even American PLACES, tourist sites and landmarks. Americans cannot be trusted with HISTORY, they have no understanding of it, they do not really BELIEVE in the past. Also, they have no TASTE.

He became incensed by American PRODUCE ('You call this a tomato?') and started growing his own chard and coriander in the back yard, as well as onions, carrots and potatoes, eventually buying a plot of land outside of town where he planted an APPLE ORCHARD. But he was a sucker for Special Offers and would often come home, chagrined, bearing five hundred rolls of toilet paper or the biggest box of Quaker Oats you ever saw.

Ferdinand was their first child. Having children is always a mistake, leading to destruction and dismay, but they didn't know that. They were happy together and thought they could EXPAND on this, take the PRINCIPLE of happiness and start multiplying.

Ferdinand turned out to be some kind of GENIUS, whom they were obliged to NURTURE. It's a bit like giving birth to Christ. He played with an abacus (MATH-EMATICALLY) at six months, read at two, made sage comments at three. Maisy and Sam fretted over his diet, his education (BEGGING teachers to be kind), and his dubious social skills. They worked themselves into a FRAZZLE over Ferdinand.

The narcissism of parenthood duly gratified, they could have stopped there but DIDN'T: they had Dot. Though not exceptional in any way, Dot was a very agreeable baby. She would sometimes wake to find the whole family STARING at her. They were entranced by her plump legs and blonde curls! Delighted with such an audience, Dot would kick her legs in the air and do a sort of prostrate JIG for them.

What is the point of child-bearing? People act like their child is their own personal DESIGN for the perfect person, but actually they have little control over what the kid becomes. Dot in her diaper, barely a blob herself, is already in charge of three hundred and forty-two eggs! Whether she uses them or not, she'll still be a DOT, as will her offspring. Death doesn't matter if we accept this. If we accept this, NOTHING matters. Even PLANTS are obsessed with SEX. The female cycad constantly thinks, WE MUST MAKE MORE OF THESE.

DOT'S INFANCY

We have our allotted era and our allotted company to keep. But such a LONG life, and each time Dot got this mean Grandma named Yetta, all alligator shoes and matching bag and a mouth like a VANILLA POD. How many whales died to daub those lips?

Yetta liked to tidy, to vacuum, to send dust into sunbeams in a way that perturbed Dot. Ferdinand was enlisted to help with the housework, washing dishes in a plastic basin on the floor while Dot shat in a corner.

Yetta was always trying to SEPARATE Dot and Ferdinand. One minute Dot would be sitting beside him, the next she was TEN FEET AWAY, facing in the opposite direction! It was baffling. Dot sometimes played POSSUM, lying very still in the hope of being left alone, or hid under beds where she examined carpets and saw the life of bugs.

Yetta once found her blue in the face, strangled by a telephone cord wrapped around her neck. Another time, Dot got caught up in the strings of the Venetian blinds at Yetta's apartment and choked! Once Dot tried to cook. She'd seen her mother pull things out of the fridge so SHE tried. A lot of stuff fell on her and it HURT. Yetta ran in with Ferdinand and shouted 'Look at you!' and dragged Dot over to the sink. Embarrassed to be scolded in front of Ferdinand, Dot watched the vanilla pod open and shut, and wondered, What's the point of grandmas? After the blood was washed off, Dot was locked in a room with Pepito, the big brown poodle. He licked her tears and let her curl up beside him to sleep.

Slow to start walking, Dot identified with dogs. She thought SHE might be a dog. It was a shock when she figured out that Pepito couldn't SPEAK. After that she noticed other things about him. His nose was awfully long, his fur very thick, and his feet small and pointy. She was not a dog – though Yetta sometimes treated her like a dog, pulling her along the street screaming, 'LEAVE IT!' when Dot tried to pick something up off the side-walk.

WHAT MADE YETTA? Nobody knows. But there are WITCH women in the world who want BAD THINGS to happen, and it WORKS.

The woman had no IMAGINATION. She'd made Sam wear a SLEEP-HARNESS until he was THIRTEEN because he'd once fallen out of bed. The sleep-harness totally IMMOBILISED him. She gave him GEFILTE FISH, cheese knoedel and peculiar Slavic delicacies to eat, and told him matzobrei is the same as French Toast. It ain't. She also wrote rhyming couplets about ZOO ANIMALS and, when not belittling Sam, fussed about the SCHWARTZEN next door, who seemed to Yetta to be procreating on a massive scale.

She had destroyed Sam's father with UNEASE before Sam was even born, ridiculing him into an early heart attack. She immediately changed her name from Weiselberg to RADZIWILL, which she'd just seen in some fashion mag. Sam resented this later, convinced his psychoanalytic career would have been aided by the name Weiselberg (it sounded WISE), but he never complained. He spent his life ducking her scorn.

She supported them by working as a dental hygienist. She never SHUT UP about teeth, judging everybody by the state of their teeth and at the least provocation advising them on dental care. Sam suspected that she would let violent criminals off lightly if their teeth were good.

Yetta sent Sam off to college in one of his father's old moth-balled suits, drastically altered, saying his father would be proud. This was not true. Sam's father would NOT have been proud to see Sam go off to college. He hadn't WANTED children, he'd wanted a DIVORCE (and he never liked that suit).

Years later Dot watched her poor crumpled father tramp through the house in muddy boots, the Big Provider, lugging his home-grown potatoes and parsnips and purple cauliflowers down to the basement where Dot and Ferdinand could roll on them. He grew melons too. Buttercups and snapdragons grew by themselves, and there was a tree in the backyard with woven, criss-crossing bark. Long strands of bark buckled other strands on to the trunk. Dot couldn't understand how the top layers stayed ON and kept trying to pull them off.

Her mother baked star-shaped cookies with coloured DOTS on them. Dot knew she was special because of these cookies. They filled the house! CLIFFS of cookies, piled HIGH, growing brittle then soggy, on every shelf. Some with raisins, some without. No one ever seemed to make a DENT in this cookie cornucopia, no matter how many they ate.

In winter, Dot and Ferdinand would put on one-piece SNOWSUITS and go out into big dots of snow. Ferdinand built himself an igloo once, when Dot was very young. She crawled in and then crawled desperately OUT. She looked up and saw blue sky moving dizzyingly around and around.

GEORGE WASHINGTON AS A BABY

There are BEAUTIFUL DAYS in America. Americans are seduced DAILY, weakened, made pliable, by the beauty of that sky. THIS is what American children really pledge allegiance to at school every day, hands on hearts. They don't just get GLIMPSES of it. They see it all day through school windows, during recess and on the way home. It continues to corrupt all day, the deep piercing blue of that old sky.

The early years at school in America are devoted to confidence, continence, nap-time, play-time, story circles, show-and-tell, reading, writing, drawing, singing, and the celebration of one goddam public holiday after another. The preparations are EXTREME. Weeks are spent constructing identical Mother's Day cards, three-dimensional Hallowe'en lanterns, pictures of Thanksgiving turkeys (made by tracing around your own hand), Christmas tree ornaments involving glitter, felt and sequins, pink tissue-paper Valentine cards and Easter crap.

Children are not being FOBBED OFF with all this

creativity because they're not smart enough yet for Calculus, nor is it anything to do with HAND-EYE CO-ORDINATION. We intensively train children in the Arts and ritual because deep down we know that these are the only things that really MATTER. This is what we must share first with the young, in case they DIE. Until Science can actually PREVENT death, it's got nothing on the Arts and ritual (although there isn't a single ritual you don't at some point wish to DEFY).

On Dot's first Hallowe'en, Ferdinand was Zorro and Dot was a cloud – she was stuffed into a pillowcase full of cotton wool with cardboard raindrops pinned all over it. They got as far as the next-door neighbours' house where they were offered PUMPKIN PIE. Dot LOVED it. She had never had pumpkin pie before. The only problem was her raindrops kept getting in the way.

At Thanksgiving every year, Dot and her family and a few of her father's ex-patients would sit around a turkey wondering what Thanksgiving's really ABOUT.

For Chanukkah, Dot and Ferdinand lit small yellow candles in the menorah that Yetta had insisted on giving them, and opened presents from her for seven nights running, mostly lousy stuff like PYJAMAS and handkerchiefs (but once, a doll that TALKED), each night a bigger but not necessarily better present, and a slightly more substantial COIN, tucked in a little envelope.

In revenge, at Christmas, Sam would make a huge gingerbread house, TWO FEET HIGH, with sugar icicles hanging from the rafters, roof tiles made of m&ms, vanilla-wafer window shutters, a chocolate door-knob and a WITCH woman standing just inside. A candied fruit path led round to the back. Dot and Ferdinand picked at all this for months, sucking at the gutters and pulling chunks off, until finally kicking at it until it collapsed.

For Easter they decorated hollowed-out eggs, by drawing on them with delicate wax-melting implements and dyeing them. On Easter morning they had an indoor JELLY-BEAN hunt but that was it – no ham, no bunny.

Ferdinand wanted to enter a float in the 4th of July Parade. The theme that year was George Washington. Ferdinand decided to do a float called: 'George Washington as a Baby'. They got the old bassinet down from the attic, decorated it with red, white and blue crêpe paper and tinsel tassels and in it laid an effigy of the infant president.

They were sure they'd win a prize but DIDN'T. On the day, they trudged TWO-AND-A-HALF MILES, maybe THREE, with the bassinet strapped on to a toy wagon which Ferdinand pulled, stopping every few paces to blow his bugle (Ferdinand in red breeches and white knee socks, Dot in a hooped skirt made by their mother). They kept George Washington in his bassinet for years afterwards, lured friends up to the attic to see the founding father there.

They had an AMERICAN CHILDHOOD in SUB-URBIA, what can I tell you? There was popcorn. There were toasted marshmallows. There were sprinklers, sparklers, dinner rolls, pickles, popsicles, icicles, grazed knees, glass in the foot, goldfish in a bag from the fair, vacant lots, school glue, car trips, Girl Scout cookies, breezes, one attempt at fishing, swings that went frighteningly high amongst oak trees, a giant cement TUBE to crawl through in some distant unfamiliar park, chipped teeth, bloody noses and MOTHERS WHO WERE ALWAYS AT HOME.

Dot and Ferdinand presented Pepito at the school Pet Show. He got Honourable Mention! They watched Saturday morning cartoons together, eating cereal. They put on plays, went skating, peeled bits of paintwork off the skirting boards, went on picnics and bicycled round and round the school playground on weekends when nobody else was there.

Between cracks in the sidewalk outside their house, Ferdinand found fossilised SHELLS. He told Dot they were trillions of years old. Weird things, curled and curlicued like time itself. What to DO with all the fossils in the world? Impossible to either find them all, or get RID of them.

Dot's IRRITATION when she came home from school, to find her mother smoking, reading and wearing glasses, or SEWING something, when she should have been thinking about DOT. Her ELATION when her mother was in the kitchen baking cookies and ready to hear which teacher had been mean. Sighting her mother's soft shoulders and yellow hair through the open back door.

The SECURITY of staying out late on summer nights after supper, running wild with the neighbour kids, knowing her mother was home. The INSECURITY of leaving her, to stay over at some friend's house where Dot wouldn't dare suck her thumb, or going off on the school bus to some MUSEUM. Missing your mother! What a great thing to HAVE, a mother. She knew Dot's favourite MEAL: French Onion Soup and Apple Pie.

Because of her mother, Dot loved that house and her own tiny room with her mother's sewing machine perched (temporarily) on the desk. Dot kept her baby pillow, slept with it so much it had to be replaced with a NEW Little Pillow but Dot weathered this. On her bed, the quilt her mother had made from many old dresses, its tight ruffled discs. The closet with its squeaky door-knob, filled with old toys and unknown family stuff like HAT BOXES. On the bedside table her electric alarm clock with its orange glow that comforted Dot at night, when all she could see outside were tiny dots of light like stars from the windows of neighbouring houses, or during TORNADO SCARES, when the sky for once was not blue but ominously yellow-grey.

THE WHOLLY IRRELEVANT
YEAR OF THE BARBECUE

There are events which CHANGE LIVES. For Dot it was the arrival of a BARBECUE JOINT in town. It just opened one day smelling of barbecue sauce and serving barbecued stuff and everyone liked it! Dot's family ate there so often it coloured the whole year for Dot. For the whole family. The whole TOWN.

It just seemed to appear one day. A whole new log cabin-style building was built for it. The chairs and tables were made from huge chunks of log too. It just opened one day smelling of its own particular brand of BAR-BECUE SAUCE, enticed everyone into its dark wooden interior to eat barbecued meat with barbecue sauce on it and chunky French fries and Coke and root beer and corn cobs and salad and coleslaw on the side, filled the TOWN with that smell and messed up the sidewalk out-side with plastic platters and forks and scraps of ham-burger bun and gnawed RIBS and onion rings in the gutter, fed everyone in town on barbecued meats and bar-becue sauce and big chunky potatoes until the walls of the restaurant were SATURATED with the smell of barbecue sauce and everybody in there was SICK of barbecue sauce and barbecued meat and chunky potatoes and coleslaw on the side. Everyone OVERDOSED on barbecued meat and barbecue sauce. For a year everyone WELCOMED the barbecue joint, tried every dish, talked about it on the way home (though you could barely WALK after eating there), went back again. Then – NO! NO MORE, sick of the sight of it, sick of the smell of it, sick of the THOUGHT of it, never want to smell that smell again or see that food.

And that was that! The place shut down. This is what HAPPENS. People take you up, embrace you, welcome you, DROWN you in their own particular brand of BARBECUE SAUCE and then they drop you, no explanation offered!

There's no knowing just how that barbecue joint, that barbecue taste, that barbecue smell and that eventual barbecue FAILURE affected everyone in town. BUT IT MUST HAVE.

THE BEST GAME IN TOWN

In the attic, near George Washington as a Baby, Dot found an old corset with fluffy edges, which reminded her of Rowlandson (her parents had a book of Rowlandson prints). She showed the corset to Ferdinand. Ferdinand painted a pubic triangle on Dot and lines on her chest suggesting breasts and thus they developed their cheerful form of rumpy-pumpy. They were not as PLUMP as Rowlandson would have liked but they had gusto and merriment. Ferdinand cried 'Wench!' while he fucked Dot boisterously from behind.

At first they didn't suspect the IN-OUT routine; they thought you just put the dick inside and left it there a while. But they soon made their own improvements on the basic PLUG idea. It was PLAY, the best indoor game they'd ever found, better than TIDDLY WINKS or Snakes & Ladders or even Monopoly (ANYTHING's better than Snakes & Ladders). How close they felt afterwards, sitting at the kitchen table competing against each other in drawing contests (no Rowlandson now, just a tree, a camel, a kangaroo), or doing their homework.

It was a trusty source of fun, but they didn't crave it in between. In fact they often FORGOT they were lovers, forgot they'd gone beyond the ginger touching of tongues so repulsive to parents, or sneaking peeks at each other through a crack in the bathroom door. They kept it secret, even from themselves.

Over the years they elaborated on the original conception, adjusting to real pubic hair and real breasts without difficulty. Caught in a sudden thunderstorm when they were alone at the orchard one day, picking apples, they had to shelter in the old corrugated-iron shed. Dot idly squeezed Ferdinand's dick until it PUSHED BACK. There on the damp ground, rain pounding hard on the roof, Ferdinand fucked Dot until she came in a new way, lengthily, LOUDLY. It astonished them both but was instantly incorporated into their repertoire.

It was sex without a single PROBLEM. No distaste, for they were family. No disapproval, for they were equally guilty. No big surprises, since they invented it together. No agenda, for there seemed to be no future. No THOUGHT, only the familiar touch, a continuing AGREEMENT that needed no revision. Like rain on a corrugated roof: a simple perfect thing.

ONIONS & LEMONS

INSECTS OUTWEIGH US. Chickens outnumber us four to one! The present human population of the earth could fit into Lake Windermere! There is liquid everywhere, running through the body, through the buildings, down the hills, streaming always downwards, muddy bloody water running through the body and the land.

What do you do if you have a fatal disease? If it's not KILLING you yet, you pretend it's not there. Your disease humiliates you, so you try not to think about it. But you're already HALF-DEAD just from KNOWING about it! You are already shutting down operations, not BOTHERING with stuff. You are already preparing yourself for losing and leaving everything.

At first Maisy was stoical, in the grand heroic tradition. She told no one, rested secretly, canned fruit, made pies, tearfully sorted through papers when nobody else was around. INCENSED that she and her concerns would soon amount to NOTHING, she embroidered. The cushion covers piled up, enough cushion covers to last her family and their descendants for centuries (as if THEY wouldn't die too). She suffered and felt virtuous in her hiding of it, got OFF on this, her only comfort. But it was a withdrawal: she kept turning from Sam in the bed. Eventually he demanded an explanation. When she told him, he cried and BEGGED her not to die.

That night they went out and got drunk together. They talked about their life, the children, Ferdinand's gifts. They talked about their love. They talked MONEY. But the DISEASE they did not discuss, out of sheer terror (and no, you DON'T get to know what it was: this is not a course in MEDICINE).

Wandering home through the back alleys of Cincinnati, they almost tumbled over a lot of small round fruits or vegetables that lay across the alleyway, dumped from some restaurant's trash-can. They leaned over and examined them a bit, then walked on hesitantly. Maisy said she thought they were lemons. Sam thought onions. In the end he had to go back and check! As he wandered away into the darkness, he told Maisy that if they turned out to be lemons he'd take her on a second trip to Mexico.

There was a long silence while Sam scrabbled on the ground somewhere. He finally came back to Maisy, his face wet with tears, and said they were lemons. Maisy never knew if this was true but at that moment, though dying and therefore barely capable of love, she loved him yet.

They arrived in Mexico City just in time for the DAY OF THE DEAD! It could have been a FIASCO. As soon as they got out of the taxi they were confronted by paper skeletons and miniature CORPSES in tiny coffins. In the hotel they found an *ofrenda* in the front parlour, dedicated to a chambermaid's baby who had died without being BAPTISED, leaving it stuck in LIMBO and therefore amongst the first due to return for the Day of the Dead. Incense was burning by the altar, which was decorated with yellow marigolds and photos of the dead baby. Brand-new toys had been placed under it, and baby food and baby clothes. The baby was expected any minute!

Sam and Maisy put their suitcases in their quiet shuttered room and went out for something to eat. Men in women's clothing and skull masks were dancing in the street: the whole world had turned INSIDE OUT. Sam and Maisy passed stalls selling little sugar skulls and paper cut-outs of jovial death scenes. The afterlife seemed pretty much the same as THIS one: you farm, you frolic, you sing, you smile, you dance, you smoke, you carry heavy loads and you EAT. Everyone was buying or cooking food for the dead. It was all too much for Sam and Maisy. They ended up buying a bottle of wine and some bread shaped like BONES and went back to their hotel.

But the next day they were desperate for MORE Day of the Dead! After eating tortillas with beans and green chillies, they wandered into a cemetery that was being dolled up for the dead, with red and yellow flowers and a new dash of white paint on all the gravestones, which gleamed in the sun. Sam and Maisy had only ever viewed death as an INVALIDATION of a person: the dead in America are immediately VACUUMED UP by some giant suburban HOUSEWIFE IN THE SKY (there's no arguing with HER). But HERE the dead still had a presence, a MEANING. In fact, they OWNED the place!

Wary of ritual, Sam held himself back from true enjoyment of this scene, but Maisy was ENCHANTED. The secret idea she was forming of an AFTERLIFE gave her the foothold she needed to endure the agonies to come, a newfound courage and optimism which found instant expression through SHOPPING.

They went to a market where Maisy bought a colourful skirt for herself, and baskets, then four nice soup bowls for however many family dinners they had left. Tiny toy coffins too! In a junk shop they saw an old revolving lamp with the image of a steam train painted on the shade in acute perspective. The hotter the lamp got, the faster the train went round and round, spewing steam. Sam thought he could detect a faint WHISTLE too, and chugging sounds. So Maisy bought it, their train through this limbo land of death. They carried their loot back to the hotel and held each other all afternoon.

While they were away, Yetta tidied with officious sanctity, forbidding any Hallowe'en shenanigans.

'How can you dress up when your mother's sick?'

She stayed up late to combat bacteria and throw out precious stuff. All night the dishwasher and washing machine raged, clothes spinning disconsolately in the drier, every light on. In the morning Dot found all the TOWELS missing and the fridge empty.

'What, WHAT?' screeched Yetta. 'I just cleaned the place up a bit, is that so bad?'

IT WAS BAD.

LIMBO LAND

What was she dying of? She was dying, that's all. You think that if you knew what it was you could AVOID it? You could rule it out? But you do accept that it happens, people dwindle and die? They do it ALL THE TIME. They don't WANT to but they do. It will happen to you and everyone you know, in due course. Whatever the cause – disease or something else – whether or not you try to evade it. Local pollutants, evil grandmas, radiation, a vitamin deficiency, a boring job, asbestos cowboys, the stress of having a GENIUS for a son or an excess of organic produce that needs bottling. IT HAPPENS. Most people in America don't believe you die if you're good. They're wrong.

Of course you're CURIOUS. We all study illness, our own especially. Every illness reminds you of every other; every time you're sick in bed you feel like a CHILD sick in bed. You want to watch TV and be brought broth and ice-cream. Maisy became childish in her last days. She surveyed the landscape of her bedroom a thousand times, looked at it in new ways that made it GIGANTIC, unfamiliar, her hands wandering upon the quilt. Her legs now needed someone else to lift them and PUT them in the bed. Her hair was gone, her speech slurred, her face like a MOON.

The sick pound you with the fact that they are sick! New intimacies are required, abhorrent reminders of how ill they are. Dot didn't mind helping her mother off the toilet or putting on her socks and shoes, but hated and feared what these jobs INDICATED. The progress of the disease was so swift, and there was no going BACK. Each new household chore her father suggested she take on depressed Dot further. Ferdinand was off the hook: in the last year of high school, he had much serious scientific work to do. He cringed from his mother's death over his microscopes. Sam did the cooking, but Dot did most of the shopping, buying ready-made meals and secret treats for herself like Twinkies, which she ate while listening to her parents in the next room.

The whole thing was GROTESQUE, her mother lying there unable to WASH herself, her father sitting beside her ENDURING that. Every night the lonely meal without her and the dishwashing after. Everything in LIMBO waiting for the DEATH, which would bring some relief. The guilt of thinking this.

Every autumn Maisy had insisted they all get in the car and go for a drive to see Fall Colour. Sam always grumbled about it, saying there were plenty of trees right by their house, but actually he LIKED driving along listening to her exclaim about a red or golden tree they passed. But this year she didn't mention Fall Colour, and when Sam offered to take her she wouldn't GO: the pain and the painkillers dissolved her interest in anything. So he brought her red and gold and green leaves in bed.

All cosy in her bed, unwilling ever to be removed from it, Maisy dreamt that she danced with paper skeleton puppets twice her size, and once, that she was running through ankle-deep water in Mexico (but this was probably because she was thirsty).

Sally, one of Sam's ex-patients, came to help out a bit. She brought brownies from some unknown bakery that were the best brownies Dot had ever had! She shopped, took Dot to her piano lessons, and she vacuumed. One day Sally got so hot vacuuming she took her shirt off and vacuumed half-NAKED. Dot was embarrassed by all this liveliness and splendour in a house of the dead, but noted that Sally had great breasts. Dot liked having her around! Then Sally stopped coming. See what happens? People come, they vacuum, and THEN what?

After Sally's disappearance Dot went into a state of TORPOR which saw her through the death and several years after it. Her metabolic rate fell, her friendships disintegrated. She lost the ability to absorb new information or handle personal hygiene. She felt perpetually cold, hungry and lethargic, HALF-DEAD.

Before Dot's mother got sick she taught Dot things: how to eat, walk, speak, go to the bathroom, tie her shoe-laces, draw, read, paint, sew, fasten buttons, snaps, toggles, hooks-and-eyes, comb her hair, brush her teeth, put on skates or galoshes, use a knife and fork, play solitaire, put stamps on envelopes, remember the days of the week, months of the year and how many days in each month. She taught her that *i* comes before *e* except after *c*. She taught Dot how to press autumn leaves in a book, draw a cat, wear sanitary towels and bake the perfect apple pie.

AFTER she got sick, Dot's mother taught her what sick people LOOK like, how little sick people can DO for you, how aggravating OTHER people are when your mother is sick, how crass doctors and nurses can be, how PREHISTORIC death is, and that your mother is irreplaceable.

Yetta arranged the funeral with gusto – she just TOOK OVER. Sam bought what seemed much too big a tombstone, sarcophagus-style, spotted it and bought it without a word. It had a stone wreath at each corner, and her name – MARY DELANY RADZIWILL – inscribed deep in its side. No RAIN would ever wear that thing out. All joy was bound up with her bones and now they were weighed down with stone.

Ferdinand was stunned amid all the grief to be shunted off to YALE. His presence wasn't needed. It was only what Sam and Maisy had always HOPED for, but Ferdinand was hurt and went sulkily off to Yale.

Everything seemed STUPID to Dot after her mother died. Stop signs were STUPID, bicycles were STUPID, mothers driving their kids to school were STUPID, SCHOOL was stupid, world events were stupid, mayors, policemen, mailmen, dry cleaners, dogs, brothers, getting up in the morning, changing your clothes, white sugar cubes in a BOWL, and anyone else's pain. SNOW was stupid, and falling in it.

DOT GOT FAT. Dot in the universe was expanding! Fatness is a WARNING: I'm not so nice. But Dot's didn't BEGIN as a protest but as a perceived NECES-SITY: nobody was feeding her! For lack of a mother she fed herself. And for lack of a mother, she recompensed herself with food. How much recompense was RE-QUIRED, to assuage the loss of a mother? Dot ate until she felt sick, then ate some more. Despite having a psychoanalyst ON THE PREMISES, Dot began to hate herself.

She had VIOLENT THOUGHTS, longed for every-thing to go WRONG for everybody, wanted the world to be even WORSE. When she saw a dam, she wanted it to collapse. When she was in a store, she hoped it would be raided by armed robbers. She longed for fire, flood, famine, BIG NEWS ITEMS. None of the disasters on offer could satisfy her.

One day, Dot lay down on her bed, having decided to DIE. From looking at her mother in her coffin, Dot knew how to die, and how to LIE, hands across the chest. She was wearing her favourite jeans. If *rigor mortis* set in, she could be dumped straight into the grave just the way she was (she'd left instructions to that effect in the suicide note under her alarm clock).

But, though fat and furious, Dot was also fourteen, fairly healthy, and she hadn't bothered to avail herself of an actual SUICIDE METHOD. So she didn't die. Instead, at 6:00 Yetta yelled for her to come to dinner and Dot hauled herself off the bed to go eat cold boiled chicken and green beans (which Yetta considered slimming). Dot added an angry amount of salt. I COULD HAVE DIED TODAY, she thought, and nobody would have CARED. She was right. Ferdinand was gone, her father had retreated to his Den to paint pointillist pictures of her mother (a little like de Kooning but done with dots), and Yetta merely upbraided Dot for crying CROCODILE TEARS and blamed everything on her mother for SMOKING.

DESTRUCTION AND DISMAY

The garden went into shock, became MORIBUND. Peas died on the vine unpicked. Birds, skunks, squirrels, chipmunks, raccoons and possums came and ate everything. Later it rallied though, giving up its vegetable functions, and burst forth with dandelions.

Pepito died. Pets always die at the WORST TIME, when no one is looking after them properly. It's INTOLERABLE. Pepito had fits, writhing on the floor, wetting himself. Sam took him to the vet and that was the end of him! (Animals are also never allowed to die NATURALLY.)

For lack of a clear refusal, Yetta moved in permanently 'to take care of things', alligator shoes tapping, mouth snapping. She was always ordering Dot around. She cleaned as if she hoped to rid the place of the last TRACE of Maisy. She scrubbed floors all afternoon, pulled things out of closets, tore up photos and pieces of paper unless Dot stopped her in time. Meals were now REGULATED, a half-hour to eat and a half-hour to wash the dishes after, and the food was Matzo Ball Soup and soft flat baked NOODLES with RAISINS! Dot thought she would die of MALNUTRITION. Nobody was taking care of her. She missed Ferdinand. She missed her mother. She missed PEPITO.

Dot went to the library and got out all the books they had on near-death experiences and paranormal phenomena. She was waiting for her mother (or Pepito) to reappear and SAVE her.

She felt her father was ACTING dead, always locked in his Den painting and listening to Bessie Smith, or staring at the revolving steam-train lamp. He was probably DYING OF MALNUTRITION. Dot brought him cheese-on-toast one day but he wasn't there. She saw his paintings stacked against the wall and decided to have a look. The pointillist phase was OVER. These were wild, nearly abstract pictures of breasts, thighs, lips and high heels, the paint wrenched down the canvas, always downwards. Across each picture he'd scratched deep the word: 'LIMBO'.

Dot had HAD it. She stomped to her bedroom, collected all the money she had and a few duds and LEFT, planning never to return. She stomped along the highway towards Cincinnati. Anyone WALKING in suburbia provokes honking and the throwing of beer cans. One guy yelled 'Whore!' from his pick-up truck. Why does every man need his own stupid TRUCK? thought Dot.

She hitched to New Haven. It took her three days, but Dot was fuelled by fear and fury and hardly noticed. She stayed at Howard Johnsons on the way. Nobody seemed to care. She was not raped or murdered. She got a HEADACHE but recovered.

Ferdinand was surprised to see her and called home immediately to tell them where she was. Dot heard her father ask if such a visit would interfere with Ferdinand's studies. He doesn't care about MY studies, she thought, and it was true – her parents had never expected much of Dot.

Dot hid in Ferdinand's room for a while, eating food he brought her like a DOG and watching him read his science books. But nobody much cared who was in the dorm, they were too busy smoking dope and protesting against the Vietnam war. Ferdinand had no FRIENDS to bother them. So Dot got braver, going out for walks in a long hippie skirt she'd bought for herself, dotted with little mirrors. At night she'd meet Ferdinand in a base-ment bar to drink jugs of beer.

She soon figured New Haven out: there's an East Rock and a West Rock and a train station in between with trains to New York, that's all you really need to know. Dot and Ferdinand would go to New York every month or two for the DAY. She also snuck into a few Yale lec-tures and Women's Lib meetings. The rest of the time, they ate pizza and pursued a quiet life, in unspoken imi-tation of their parents.

Sex became so automatic, Dot no longer thought about it. No longer noticed Ferdinand lying down beside her, merely knew and liked the feel of him there. How could she not come to rely on that warmth, assume it to be hers, TAKE it? A nightly business, like sleep, without consequence. They never SPOKE of it. They were a living breathing TABOO! They didn't stand around waiting to sign AFFIDAVITS. They knew how UNAMERICAN it was, to take sex beyond the aerobic WORK-OUT it's supposed to be and make it meaningful.

Everything was hunky-dory in fact, until Yetta called one day to say their father was sick. Dot and Ferdinand caught the next plane to Cincinnati and went straight to the hospital where they found their father MORIBUND. Self-neglect, said the doctor, but Dot suspected malnutrition (YETTA'S doing). He revived enough though, when Ferdinand took his hand, to lean forward and say conspiratorially, 'The name . . . is . . . Weiselberg.'

Dot and Ferdinand had no idea what he was TALKING about. To Yetta's vexation, he repeated it, gasping, 'The name is Weiselberg!' before dropping back on the pillow. Then he stopped BREATHING. Ferdinand pumped his father's chest in an attempt to save him, but he died (secretly hoping there's an afterlife).

Yetta took over the funeral arrangements, burying Sam in a brand-new Jewish cemetery with room left over beside him for HERSELF. Dot and Ferdinand were left to sort out his affairs: papers, paintings, tax stuff, bank stuff, Death Certificates, magazine subscriptions - remnants of a life. (Curiously, no mention of the name WEISELBERG anywhere, leaving their father's last words a mystery.)

At night they lay in each other's arms, shocked to be orphans, listening to odd creaks and thumps in the Den, which they assumed were YETTA, cleaning. They were wrong. It was their father's GHOST in the Den, searching exasperatedly for his Birth Certificate, the ORIGINAL not a photocopy, and Yetta was outside their DOOR. Ferdinand's room had a lock so they'd always considered themselves safe in there, but Yetta had a bunch of keys she'd found in the basement during one of her big Spring Cleans and she opened the door with EASE. Dot and Ferdinand jumped out of bed but that didn't help: they were NAKED. They hoped she might faint, or DIE, at the sight, but Yetta TRIUMPHED, grabbing Dot by the hair and tugging her out of the room. Ferdinand was sent straight back to Yale, and within days Dot was at the doctor's, where it was decided she was PREG-NANT (just as Yetta had predicted). An abortion was coldly arranged, Yetta driving Dot from one appointment to another, haranguing and harassing her.

'Incest. INCEST. Such a crime.'

It was quite a while before Dot thought up her mumbled reply: 'Who did it hurt?' But Yetta had never listened to a thing Dot said and she didn't listen now. She was trying to concentrate on her driving. She shouldn't have been driving AT ALL. She was shaking with fury and she could only see out of one eye. But if it meant killing a cat, or driving into someone's trash-can, so be it, as long as she was able to get Sam's delinquent daughter to the abortion clinic on time.

Dot's humiliation seemed complete, but wasn't! New facts emerged during the abortion, of a physiological, gynaecological, ILLOGICAL nature: Dot had two vaginas and two wombs.

A double hysterectomy was immediately carried out,

neither womb being considered viable. But the surgeons left the two vaginas (they constituted no risk to health) and left Dot to her disgust. She couldn't believe she'd been carrying all these ORGANS around without knowing it. Female genitalia are weird enough; it was hard on Dot to have the WEIRDEST.

On hearing the news, Ferdinand had a nervous breakdown. He had to skip half a semester. Not only had he been caught fucking his SISTER, by his GRAND-MOTHER, with his FATHER lying fresh in his grave, but she had TWO VAGINAS and he hadn't even NOTICED. He was supposed to be a GENIUS.

First the shiksa wife, now the disastrous daughter. Where had Sam gone wrong? Yetta wondered. But she had a PLAN, a punitive plan (the modern equivalent of a convent!).

As soon as Dot could WALK again, Yetta proposed that she go to CHARM SCHOOL and learn something about the REAL WORLD. Full of self-loathing, Dot agreed to this immediately. She could think of nothing better than to devote herself to charm.

So Dot proceeded onwards. It was a HABIT.

DOT THE BODY

Armed with diet pills, lingering abdominal pains, gynae-cological peculiarities, and an uncomfortable underwire bra, Dot went off to Dallas which offered the toughest, meanest, most UNCOMPROMISING Charm School in the country, perhaps the UNIVERSE.

Dot was taught how to sit upright on a chair, stand, carry a book on her head, get in and out of a car grace-fully, and bow to royalty, including WHICH ONES to bow to (some only deserve a wave). She learnt that she too could have a flawless back, that one should always dine on fish, wear hats at an angle, lick the glass before drinking (to avoid lipstick marks), and apply mascara to each eyelash INDIVIDUALLY. She learnt that glamour doesn't come easy, beauty comes from within, cleavage and chiffon don't mix, perfume once opened lasts six months, the double-breasted look is very hard to get right, red and orange should never be worn together, stilettos should be worn with pride, gin and vodka have half the calories of beer and wine, and butter is LIQUID FAT.

Dot went to classes in: How To Wake Up Looking Gorgeous, How To Wear Grey, and Kissable Hair: How To Get It. She was taught how to find a RICH MAN, and how to make a (rich) man happy. Magazines, for instance. Never leave a load of magazines on the FLOOR. Men HATE that. Roll them up, tie them with string and stand them upright in a box (the mags, not the men).

They taught Dot everything they knew! She had her teeth capped, her body buffed, and her pubic hair SHAPED. They starved and sculpted her, these experts who somehow never TIRE of the human body or lose track of how they think it ought to look.

Dot learnt that the perfect and the beautiful have to deal with shit and snot too – the trick is to make it seem EFFORTLESS.

There is water running through the body, through the land. Dot was told to drink two litres of it a day.

She was a receptive pupil. It takes a certain type of person to put up with this sort of crap, but DOT WAS THAT TYPE. A nice sharp-nosed blonde can do very well in Dallas with the right training. One day, walking through a Mall at her most wan, Dot was spotted by a CHEEKBONE connoisseur and invited to become a MODEL. Modelling work was one of the highest ambitions formulated at Dot's Charm School (the others being Beauty Queen or First Lady). Dot leapt at the chance, in fact she leapt a little inelegantly at the CONNOISSEUR, but only because she was delirious from malnutrition. Within days she had been welcomed into the fucked-up world of FASHION.

At seventeen and now weighing only 88 lbs., Dot was almost too fat and old to BE a model. But her enervation won acclaim, and the name Radziwill was a help. Dot was posed, poked and prodded until she produced IMAGES FOR OUR TIME.

She found it hard at first to get used to the attitude of her fellow models to designers, squealing like TARTS about their PIMPS. They had FAKE ORGASMS just saying the NAMES: 'Oh, Lagerfeld . . .' 'Oooh, Yves Saint Laurent, isn't he GREAT?' they drooled. They starved, simpered and SUFFERED to please these guys, who in turn had fake orgasms thinking about all the ART they could buy with the money. Full of contempt for women, they promoted: THE BOYISH LOOK.

But just how baby-soft does skin have to BE, how concave the female abdomen? In all this glorification of youth and beauty, what happens to the MIDDLE-AGED? In all the sickening concentration on CHILDREN (really a form of paedophilia) and CHILDHOOD (so beloved of psychoanalysts), all this IDEALISATION of children – their needs, their desires, their EQUIPMENT – what about US, what about the middle-aged? WE'RE the ones who are scared and alone.

REMOVING THE THYMUS

While Dot was reaching the pinnacle of her effectiveness at WEARING CLOTHES, Ferdinand was gaining prominence at Yale. His scientific interests had been rewarded with fellowships, grants, and honorary degrees! Recognising him as some kind of Zoology GENIUS, Yale had given him a professorship, his own lab, and NO ADMINISTRATIVE DUTIES. Ferdinand had it MADE.

His main focus was the study of marsupials, which he considered a much-maligned branch of the mammalian tree. In numerous badly written articles in scientific journals, Ferdinand had questioned the lowly status of marsupials, arguing that since they had somehow SURVIVED for millions of years, their evolutionary choices (such as the pouch) must have some validity. The truth was Ferdinand just loved pouches. What could be better than a built-in BAG in which to feed, shelter and transport progeny? How many other animals come equipped with their own CARRY-COT? What a great IDEA.

So Ferdinand pottered around his lab studying marsu-pials. How we love animals in cages! There is nothing so deeply pleasing to a carnivore as seeing a lot of prey caged, especially if they're ALPHABETICALLY ARRANGED (the reason we like wildlife shows on TV so much is that the TV set looks like a cage!). Specimens were shipped dead or alive from Australia for him. He studied the anatomy, social structure and behaviour of the Kangaroo (Red and Grey), the Koala, the Quokka, the Cuscus, the Tammar, the Bandicoot, the Great Glider, the Fat-Tailed Dunnart, the Wombat and the Wallaby. Then there was a hiccup in funding. Ferdinand was forced to investigate a cheaper source of supply. He quickly settled on the Virginia Opossum. They were abundant in his native land. In fact they were, to speak unscientifically here for just a moment, A DIME A DOZEN, particularly in the southern states, though they ranged as far north as Ohio. Ferdinand had seen a dead one once in the gutter near his home. He'd been impressed by the THUMBS on its back feet, and for years had assumed the word 'opossum' was some kind of elision of 'opposable thumb'. Anyway, if Ferdinand didn't buy them they'd only get skinned for their fur or put into Possum Stew (or BOTH), and though Ferdinand TRIED to be unsentimental about animals, he really hated hearing about marsupials being EATEN.

So he cleared the lab of its dead and refilled it with possums, their funny ears and crocodile mouths pointing at him from all directions as he carried on his IMPOR-TANT SCIENTIFIC WORK of removing and dissect-ing things in order to determine which bits of its anatomy the Virginia Opossum can do WITHOUT, and for how long. There was no knowing how this information could ever be used for the good of HUMANITY or anybody else. It was pursuit of knowledge FOR ITS OWN SAKE. Hoorah!

Ferdinand studied the opossum STOMACH, finding it to be deeply sacculated. He studied opossum chromosomes (very low karyotype), their pituitary glands (necessary for follicular growth and ovulation), their diet (omnivorous). He explored the thermoregulatory influence of the hypothalamus by placing fine electrodes on it and evoking behavioural responses through electrical stimulation. He tested the dehydration rate of embryonic possums in the pouch by taking them off the teat and checking how long they survived. He examined opossum kidney function (relatively thick medulla and nephrons with loops of Henle) and found that their renal concentration ability was inferior to that of other marsupials. But their immunological competence was good: if inflicted with a dirty wound, infants under seven days old couldn't fight it, but over that age they COULD. The development of lymphoid tissue was grossly affected by removing the thymus when the creature was a week old.

He studied the pampiniform plexus, the adrenal cortex and the masticatory apparatus (molars), and did some well-regarded research on the opossum brain, comparing it to the HUMAN brain – Ferdinand found the opossum brain to be inferior. In opossums, the fore brain is divisible into an anterior telencephalon and posterior diencephalon and the hind brain is divisible into an anterior metencephalon and posterior myelencephalon. For the purposes of motor function the axons of large neurons pass via the corpus striatum and the cerebral peduncles. Ferdinand concluded that opossums are stupider than us because: A) they have no clear ability to think, either in abstract terms, or in terms of the past, present and future; B) they have no ability to PLAN; C) they have no decipherable language; and D) they have no art. (He left out our capacity for BITCHING, SWINDLING and WAR.)

Ferdinand explored the opossum's ability to 'play possum' when shaken by a predator (Ferdinand). He also investigated 'torpor' (the opossum's particular brand of hibernation) by drastically lowering the temperature in the lab – those who refrained from torpor died.

The bifurcated penis, *behind* rather than in front of the testicles, seemed to Ferdinard to correspond in some way to the idiosyncracies of the marsupial female's urogenital tract, in which the cloacal opening splits into two vaginae halfway up. This was linked to his ongoing study of the developing EMBRYO from its earliest stages: he had found out that within the limits of the embryo and for a short distance beyond, the mesoderm splits into two layers, the somatic mesoderm being applied to the ectoderm and the splanchnic mesoderm to the endoderm.

Ferdinand was splicing through his eighth female urogenital system of the day in search of embryos, and holding two little opossum uteri in his hand, when he finally realised what he was DOING: he was experimenting on DOT. Inside these sagging corpses, he had actually been seeking DOT's interior decor and furnishings. She had inspired all of his research, in fact Dot and Dot alone had made Ferdinand the world-renowned scientist he was! (He did not stop to consider WHY Dot's genitalia resembled an opossum's, nor to blame her for not having a pouch.)

With a jolt, he realised he LOVED her and that everything he had done for the last three years had been WRONG. He shouldn't have listened to Yetta, he should have stayed with Dot – ALWAYS! They could have lived quietly together in some suburb, no one would know. It was ABSURD that he had given Dot up. For WHAT? Yetta? SCIENCE? There is no point in Science! It's all guff, he knew that now.

Seized by a sudden sense of his own futility, stupidity, and unquenchable BEREFTITUDE, Ferdinand turned his scalpel on himself and DIED, much to the bewilderment of his docile possum audience. A great scientific mind lost to humanity.

But what good would it have done if he'd lived? A few more short articles on marsupials, starting with a summary, an introduction, and a discussion of methods and theories, followed by findings and an abrupt conclusion, would have appeared in the *Aust. J. Zool.*, or the *Proc. Linn. Soc. N.S.W.* or the *J. Mammal* or the *Am. anat. Mem.* or the *C.S.I.R.O. Wildl. Res.* or, if he was lucky, maybe the *Univ. Calif. Publs. Zool.*

BIG DEAL.

DOTS ON THE BODY

Blusher was being applied to the APPLES of Dot's cheeks in preparation for some stupid FASHION SHOOT, when Yetta phoned her. At first it was hard to make any sense out of Yetta's babbled tirade, zooming by electronic means to Dot in Dallas. But the gist was that it was all Dot's FAULT.

'Such a LOSS TO HUMANITY . . . a great scientific mind . . . could have SAVED LIVES . . . lost, LOST, all because of YOU and your . . . You DESTROYED him . . .'

Dot dropped the phone, sank to the floor and burst into tears. This meant the poor make-up artist (a legendary GENIUS) would have to start from SCRATCH when Dot calmed down! Foundation, mascara, eye-liner, lipstick, lip-liner, blusher – the LOT. And it was ALL DOT'S FAULT.

Red Dot. On floor. Kleenex brought. The noise. The NOSE. Assumptions made. Boyfriend. Dumped? AWWWW.

But Dot had no BOYFRIENDS. She had only Ferdinand. She had wanted no other, and had been WAITING for him all this time. It was YETTA's fault he'd died, Yetta's fault they'd been separated. For THREE YEARS Dot had longed for him, longed for their life together to resume – a simple perfect thing.

Now we'll never be together. I'll never kiss him again, never sleep beside him. How could he do it? Didn't he know we would be together again some day?

Dot returned to Cincinnati for yet another funeral organised by Yetta. The woman PRESIDED OVER DEATH. But Dot's plan to KILL her collapsed when she saw how decrepit Yetta was now, her skin scaly as an alligator's. She just wandered around the house, watering dead plants and looking for things she said she'd lost. She'd lost her MARBLES, Dot thought.

Rich from all her modelling work and the prospect of selling the house, Dot found Yetta a sheltered apartment in a building full of evil grandmas, kindly drunks, and paranoid busy-bodies who were always calling the POLICE (unfortunately the drunks tended to die off first). There was also a facility upstairs for the TOTALLY gaga (which Dot felt Yetta would soon need), and it was near a Mall! Refusing to believe Dot possessed either nobility or MONEY, Yetta was convinced the place was some suspicious kind of BARGAIN, but she agreed to go.

The tables had turned. Now DOT was alone, sort of widowed, and in charge of the old homestead. Dot LOVED that house. There were remnants of family life that even Yetta had not managed to WRECK. Like, hundreds of napkins printed with DOLLAR SIGNS (**$**), which Dot's father had picked up cheap somewhere. Dot fingered them, remembering her mother's refusal to use them, they were so ugly. (Her father's surprise!) There were tablecloths too that brought it all back: Sunday breakfasts on spring days with the kitchen door open, a little breeze coming in, the dangling stained-glass ornaments knocking against the window-pane.

Dot deliberated over the silver, which her mother had occasionally polished before company came. Long-forgotten, never-used kitchen accessories like lobster bibs and crab-claw crackers. The many and varied (much used) corn-cob holders, and jars, so many JARS, that her mother had once filled with jam or spaghetti sauce or star-shaped cookies – important SUPPLIES. Now all empty.

In the attic: toys, snowsuits, skates, schoolwork, rugs, cushion covers, Mexican bowls, Dot's Little Pillow (she SNATCHED that up), and George Washington as a Baby. He had aged badly: his white flannel face was peppered with what looked like BLACKHEADS or maybe SCABIES. Dot didn't dare investigate his NETHER REGIONS. She just dumped him and his bassinet straight into a trash bag. POOR infant president.

She wept in Ferdinand's room, lay on his bed thinking of their couplings, clutching his pillow. She thought of the life they'd had together, the Saturday mornings, the picnics, his patient explanations of James Bond movies, their Hallowe'en costumes, trips to the Mall, duets (Dot at the piano, Ferdinand with a series of wind instruments), the apple orchard and the corrugated-iron shed. The

ROUTE they'd negotiated together through life, their SURVIVAL (until now). She thought of the life they could have had as adults, if he hadn't abandoned her. In this same house or, if the neighbours objected, somewhere similar. Who would it have hurt?

Dot could not BEAR this loss. She lay there hoping he would return. She WAILED. She longed so much for him to return that Ferdinand was forced to obey!

Still lying there later that night, Dot heard a noise and felt him join her. All the old pleasure – she was in his arms! She touched his cheek, the cold cheek of a ghost. He tried to take her from behind.

But, for the first time, Ferdinand's body seemed ALIEN. INTRUSIVE, her hand on his thigh. UNWELCOME, his fingers in her. Everything HURT. It occurred to her that Ferdinand might have BLACK DOTS on him like George Washington as a Baby, and SHE DIDN'T WANT TO SEE THEM.

But in the morning he was gone (he couldn't preserve a corporeal form for long) and Dot wondered if it had all been a DREAM: she vaguely remembered him asking for his passport.

Dot held a garage sale on the front lawn. She sold the silver, the plastic pitcher for Kool-Aid, the tablecloths, the bowls, the rag rugs, the board games, the revolving steam-train lamp, everything her parents had planned and done and LIKED. It seemed traitorous to sell it but she did.

Neighbours Dot didn't even know came and commiserated, before making off with handy items. In a mixture of emotions that confused EVERYBODY (kindness, nostalgia, ENVY), they gathered there on the front lawn, gossiped, drank lemonade and bought things – for no suburban home's complete without a bit of what's next door.

The day of the house sale arrived. Lots of people turned up wanting to buy it. One pair had evidently rehearsed their two daughters to make a speech and sing a song. Wearing identical sailor suits and tap-shoes, the girls sang (to the tune of 'Frère Jacques'):

> We so love your
> Pretty how-owse
> With the woods
> All around.
>
> We would love it always!
> It's got pretty flowers
> In the front
> And the back.
>
> It's so quiet,
> And so peaceful.
> It's so sweet!
> It's so great!
>
> We would love it always!
> Won't you sell it to us?
> Pretty please,
> Pretty please.

A bowing and scraping tap-dance followed the song. Then the girls talked IN UNISON about how they loved to think of Dot as a little girl in that house because THEY were little girls and they thought they would be as happy as Dot in that house. Dot wanted to kill them.

Another couple saw it merely as a vacant lot. They were going to BULLDOZE the place and put up an inland LIGHTHOUSE, complete with sauna, jacuzzi, tumbleweed and shells.

YETTA turned up, offering to REINSTALL herself so that ungrateful Dot wouldn't have to sell the house. Dot stuffed her right back in her taxi, defusing her tirade with a $20 bill.

In the end the house was sold to a couple with a baby, who didn't sing, dance or bulldoze (at least in front of DOT). On a last visit to the cemetery, orphaned, widowed Dot decided to change her name to Dot de Lany, in memory of her mother. Dot was feeling indiscriminately guilty towards EVERYBODY, even the chipmunks and possums behind the old, sold house.

A SINGLE SOLITARY DOT

Sex and death are a great COMBO. No longer protected by Ferdinand, nor bound to him, let LOOSE by him in fact, and rather lost without him, Dot resolved on the plane back to Dallas that she would try her two vaginas out on the REAL WORLD. Forget catwalks and cocaine: Dot wanted COITUS. (Quick.)

She had them all! Lagerfeld, Lacroix, Ungaro, Armani, Gucci, Valentino, Dolce, Gabbana, Galliano, Versace and Calvin Klein, every time they passed through town. Dot's mumbling inquietude proved IRRESISTIBLE TO MEN. Women too! There were few female DESIGNERS around, but plenty of BEAUTY CONTESTANTS. Dot fucked (in order of seniority): Miss Fried Chicken, Miss Twinkie, Miss Xerox (all TEN of them, with decreasing satisfaction), Miss Time-Share, Miss Bare Breasts, Miss Otis Elevators (up, down, but not sideways), Miss Redneck of Tulia, Miss Dallas, Miss Grand Canyon, Miss Texas, Miss NATO, Miss America, and Miss Universe (though SHE didn't like being in Dot – she only liked Dot being in HER).

What Dot noticed most was how HOT their bodies felt. Everyone seemed much hotter than DOT. She was the WRONG TEMPERATURE. She'd lie next to her lovers scared to TOUCH them, they were so hot. But no one seemed to notice. Nor did they detect the dual vagina problem (the anterior and lateral vaginae merged fairly high up and the septum between them was barely detectable, except that knocking against it added to pleasure). In fact, everybody thought Dot was a DREAM-BOAT IN BED!

She was such a dreamboat in bed her agent suggested she try her hand at a little PORN. He knew a place in Mexico and he could set it all up. Dot could scoot down there for a few weeks, start a whole new CAREER for herself by being a dreamboat in bed, and be back in Dallas in time for her next cat-walk engagement. It seemed a small enough step, from modelling to having her ass reamed in public, so Dot was happy to go.

When she arrived at the hotel where the filming was taking place, she was sent into a dingy back room. Three big sweaty American guys were sitting around a huge metal desk. They immediately asked her to take off her clothes! But, being in the fashion industry, Dot was used to such treatment. She understood they had to see if HER breasts would fit in THEIR movie.

The hotel was empty, apart from people involved in the movie, and a Photography Club from Minnesota who were just there to WATCH. The trouble was, as soon as filming got under way the Minnesota guys said they wanted to TAKE PART, rather than merely take snapshots of OTHER guys getting laid. The director was reluctant to include them though, as they were untried as actors, and all very FAT.

The days wore on. Dot became used to the routine: it was rape, rape, rape all summer long. She never left the hotel and, alone in her room at night, she began to feel touches of ALIENATION. She ate pomegranates and dreamt of the Underworld. In the morning she'd look out of her little window, like a PRISONER, and see the perfect circles of white sheets drying on top of cacti down below, just big white DOTS to Dot. They seemed like MIRACLES of whiteness.

They were filming a torture scene in which Dot had to hang upside-down from a chandelier and suck cock. But they were having trouble with the male star's erection, despite all the efforts of the FLUFFERS (peasant girls from the neighbouring hills). Dot hung there, uncomplaining, until she heard one of the Minnesota guys begging the director to be allowed to STEP IN and SAVE THE DAY. The director, undone by the heat and general porn ENNUI, agreed! This enraged Dot, who watched upside-down as they lathered the Minnesota guy with fake tan and the fluffers started on HIM. Any minute now he'd be let loose on Dot. She had nothing against MINNESOTA, but everyone has their LIMIT.

Dot said in a commanding voice, 'Untie me, please!' Nobody listened. So she said a little louder, 'immediately! Untie me to canoodle with dumb-ass SHUTTERBUGS. Untie me I came here to be in a professional PORN MOVIE, not

Nothing.

FURIOUS at the combination of being NAKED and IGNORED, Dot tried to untie HERSELF. She shifted around, squirming, writhing and jerking helplessly, her strong little arms flailing, until the whole chandelier began to swing. The pendulum motion MESMERISED the crew. They couldn't MOVE. Viewing this as an attempt on Dot's part to scupper his embryonic porn career, the Minnesota guy made a lunge for the chain holding her hands together, but missed and fell over a low wall into the SWIMMING-POOL with a huge splash. This broke the spell. Someone went to save HIM, and the best boy released Dot.

She felt like a FREED SLAVE. Without pausing to debate with them, she ran up to her room, threw on some clothes, grabbed her money and her passport and rushed outside. For the first time she saw MEXICO: it was colourful! She walked until she reached the nearby town of Tzintzuntzán. Dot mastered the percussive name while she drank tequila at a bar. Then she went outside and wandered towards a beguiling patch of blue water: Lake Pátzcuaro. When she reached the shore she took off her shoes and RAN, ankle-deep in water, a FREED SLAVE. The human sacrifice was OVER. In the sand she found a fossilised FISH, and put it in her pocket.

She lay down near the water, thought longingly of her Little Pillow, and fell asleep. Dot dreamt she was being eaten by Yetta in thin slices, and woke up with a fright. Everything was dark. Maybe Yetta HAD eaten her. Maybe she was dead!

Dot saw stars and heard the sound of tinkling bells. It

must be HEAVEN, Dot thought (based on her rudimentary religious training), though she hadn't expected it to be so DARK.

She wanted to be officially RECEIVED in some way, she wanted ceremony, ritual, a HALO. The ground felt surprisingly solid under her when she stood up. She heard water gurgling and remembered the lake, but she could still see no division between water and land and sky. It was as if the world had turned itself INSIDE OUT. The starry sky and glittery water had merged in a vision of:

I N F I N I T Y!!!

Dead or alive, Dot stumbled along the shore, heading for a big group of stars like a GALAXY, that were jumping around oddly. As she got closer she realised that some of them were candle flames, and the candles were on BOATS. What a great IDEA. She hoped SHE'D be given a boat too. (AND a halo.)

Then she bumped into something – a MAN! God maybe? Or a dead relative? Her heart lurched at the thought. She touched him. He felt familiar – it was FERDINAND. He SMELLED like Ferdinand (Ferdinand's cinnamony smell was one of the few smells Dot knew well). But he was warm this time, not ghostly. She rested her cheek against his chest.

'Ferdinand.'

'No, but whoever he is I'm jealous!'

This man was not Ferdinand! He was ENGLISH. (He

was John Butser!) Dot had to sit down. John helped her over to a bench, hesitated, then sat down next to her – Dot's mumbling inquietude was alluring.

They sat watching the boats come and go from the pier, bobbing on the water. Dot was beginning to calm down, when there was a great hullabaloo! A man dressed as a FISH suddenly ran into the water, only to be instantly surrounded by other men with wide round fishing-nets, with which they ceremonially CAUGHT him. People cheered from the shore.

Fingering her fish fossil, Dot looked at John with his money pouch dangling in his lap. He did not look like Ferdinand, but he did have his SMELL and something of his MANNER. Perhaps this was enough? Over-whelmed by her escape from porno purgatory and by her imaginary encounter with paradise, Dot leaned over and kissed him.

The folds of her cunt were like VELVET as she milked him. She came loudly, clinging to him, and slept all night with her hand in his. Her cunt felt hot against his back, her stomach cooler. John never KNEW how passionate Dot was about him, or why. He just thought she was a DREAMBOAT IN BED. (He was very SCIENTIFIC about such things. Sex was a purely physical activity, in his opinion, best executed by skilled practitioners.)

DOT WAS IN LOVE. She had grown cold and quiet for lack of motherlove and motherland. This is nothing to do with mothers or national BORDERS, it is about having SOMEWHERE ON EARTH where you feel comfortable: A POUCH! She could LIVE in this man, cry in him, be given air and food and warmth by him.

The next morning John took her out for tamales, but they couldn't eat them, they were too much IN LOVE, so they went back again to his hotel. Later, Dot got a taxi out to her own hotel to collect her stuff. She tiptoed past the torture chamber where they were already filming with a NEW GIRL and hurried up to her room. In the corridor she met the guy from Minnesota. All animosity gone, Dot smiled at him, and he said, 'Bitch.'

Back in Tzintzuntzán Dot noticed that the bakery they'd gone to earlier for tamales had a huge painting on the window of a skeleton gobbling bread – it must be the Day of the Dead! This depressed Dot, reminding her of her parents coming home from Mexico laden with weird trinkets and good cheer, a macabre performance and the preamble to miserable days of decay and dismay.

Near the hotel she saw a crowd of small children all weeping silently, with one chubby fist rubbing their eyes, the other hand pointing down at the ground. They turned out to be STATUES, and they were for sale. Dot WANTED one! When she met up with John, she mentioned that she was going to buy one. He begged her not to.

'Why not?'

'It would be hard to lug back to England,' he said.

Dot looked at him, baffled.

'You will come, won't you?' he said, and the world turned inside out, AGAIN, for her.

They swam, ate chalupas, got sick and got married. The

registrar read them their rites in a BOOMING VOICE, as if he wanted all of Mexico to know these people were no Catholics. But maybe he was just trying to be HEARD over the mariachi band that was already strumming and drumming and screeching outside.

John never asked Dot what exactly she was doing in Mexico. He assumed she'd come for the Day of the Dead: the lake, the boats, the Fish Guy, toy coffins. Dot never asked John what HE was doing there either. What innocents! John had in fact come in the hope of breaking into the Mexican PORN scene, but couldn't find the hotel. He gave the whole idea up though, when he met Dot. He only wanted to be with HER, inside her velvet cunt, and take her back to Jaywick.

JAYWICK SANDS. It sounded idyllic to Dot, as she sat beside her magnificent hubby on the turbulent plane. Looking out at the stars, she wondered yet again about the UNIVERSE, and whether there were other forms of life out there.

She was right to wonder! As she stared out at outer space, a dot stared back at DOT.

A NOTE ON THE AUTHOR

Lucy Ellmann's previous novels are *Man or Mango?*,
Varying Degrees of Hopelessness and *Sweet Desserts*, which
won the *Guardian* Fiction Prize.

Varying Degrees of Hopelessness Lucy Ellmann
£6.99 0 7475 6272 5

'This is a novel like nothing else, an irresistible cocktail of satire, slapstick and tenderness' *Cosmopolitan*

In an eminent London art institute – the Catafalque – Our Heroine Isabel (she of the obsessional habits, perpetual virginity and peculiar belly button) sit in wistful contemplation of Chardin's brushstrokes and the virile red socks of passing lecturers. Isabel's wholly imaginary love life (based on the romantic notions of authoress Babs Cartwheel) bears little resemblance to that of her flatmate Pol, who prefers to grip reality by the balls. Enter Robert, victim of an American childhood, kitsch memorabilia, academic rivalry, Pol's belly-dancing and Isabel's mute adoration. Can he be perverse enough not to despair?

'Ellmann is an expert juggler with words ... her satire is deft, sophisticated, and enchantingly surreal' *Sunday Telegraph*

'Funny and furious ... Lucy Ellmann is clever, and very angry' *The Times*

To order from Bookpost PO Box 29 Douglas Isle of Man IM99 1BQ www.bookpost.co.uk
email: bookshop@enterprise.net fax: 01624 837033 tel: 01624 836000

bloomsburypbks

www.bloomsbury.com/lucyellmann